Anonymous

Our Centennial Memoir

Anonymous

Our Centennial Memoir

ISBN/EAN: 9783744659871

Printed in Europe, USA, Canada, Australia, Japan

Cover: Foto ©Raphael Reischuk / pixelio.de

More available books at **www.hansebooks.com**

OUR CENTENNIAL MEMOIR.

FOUNDING OF THE MISSIONS,

SAN FRANCISCO DE ASSIS

IN ITS HUNDREDTH YEAR

THE CELEBRATION OF ITS FOUNDATION.

HISTORICAL REMINISCENCES

OF THE MISSIONS OF CALIFORNIA.

—◦✧◦—

SAN FRANCISCO

COMPILED, PRINTED AND PUBLISHED BY P. J. THOMAS,

No. 505 CLAY STREET,

1877.

PREFACE.

In presenting this little volume to the public for their acceptance and approbation, the publisher does not think it necessary, or advisable, to trouble them with a lengthy preface. There are many reasons why a book like this, simple, unpretentious and purely historical in its character, should be laid before the citizens of San Francisco. They have but recently celebrated the hundredth anniversary of the foundation of their beautiful and interesting city, and it seems but right that some more enduring and substantial record than the reports, however full and complete, of newspapers, which are of their very nature but the things of a day, should be made of an event of such importance. The object of the publisher, therefore, is to contribute his humble but sincere effort towards transmitting to posterity the record of the foundation of civilization on the shores of California. If his labor meets the approval of those who participated in it, he will be amply satisfied and he will not think his toil in vain.

To give a concise narrative of the past; to depict in truthful colors the aims and objects of the devoted men who raised the banner of Christianity and of civilization where one of the greatest cities of the world is now established; to vindicate the character of the zealous missionaries to whose earnestness in the cause of the Gospel San Francisco owes its origin—these are some of the motives which prompted the compilation of the volume now laid before the public. It may serve, also, to show to those who in the coming century shall help to raise upon these foundations the grand monuments of a peerless civilization, the self-sacrifice, the Christian fortitude, the heroic perseverance of those Catholic Friars who devoted life, energies, everything they possessed to the service of their Divine Master, who knew no earthly ambition, who thought not of fame, who not even dreamt of handing down their names to the men who in after years would reap the fruits of their incessant toil.

Many efforts have been made by the noble and disinterested members of the Pioneer Association, by lectures, pamphlets, etc., to preserve the records of California's past ; but they, unhappily, were not of an enduring character. The documents remain in the libraries of the few—too few —who feel an interest in the story of the vicissitudes of the Golden City of the Pacific, and that is all. To do something towards dissipating this reprehensible and unpatriotic apathy, to construct some humble memorial of the past, is the most cherished desire of

THE PUBLISHER.

Historic Outlines.

THE Missions of California are the landmarks of its civilization. The struggles of the early missionaries, against the most appalling obstacles, to plant the Cross in a wild and unknown country, are full of interest to those who have profited by their unexampled heroism. The Jesuits, the first missionaries who succeeded in effecting a lodgment on the peninsula of California, after being expelled from Mexico in 1767, were succeeded by the Franciscans, at whose head Father Junípero Serra was placed as President of the Missions. Father Serra was a man of remarkable sagacity, energy and patience. His aim was the occupation of the whole country from San Diego to Monterey, and then proceeding northward to discover the lost bay of San Francisco, where Vizcayno claimed to have anchored in 1602, although it has since been conclusively established that Point Reyes was the limit of his explorations. Father Junípero's expedition was divided into two detachments, one of which started from Villacata by land, and the other from San Blas by sea. The march from Villacata, the frontier Mission of Lower California, occupied fifty-one days. When the explorers reached Point Pinos, they did not recognize the indentation of the coast as corresponding with Vizcayno's description, and there-fore determined to push farther northward. Accord-ing to the diary of Father Crespi, who accompanied the expedition, they halted at the point of land which shelters Half Moon Bay, now called Point Corral de Tierra, which they named Point Angel de Guarda. From here they sent out an exploring party, which returned at the end of three days, and reported that, on ascending the mountain range on their right, they had discovered an arm of the sea extending inward to the southeastward. From this elevation Point Reyes and the Farallones were visible. The entire expedi-tion, on leaving this point, started to the northeastward and continued in a course parallel to the bay, intending to pass around its head, and so reach Point Reyes. They camped near the San Francisquito creek, at the place where is now the village of Searsville. But here, their supplies being exhausted, and several of the party having died from scurvy, they resolved to retrace their steps, although Governor Portolá was disposed to push on. The homeward march was a distressing one. Their food consisted only of shellfish, acorns, pine-nuts, and the few wild birds they succeeded in shooting. On November 27th they arrived at Point Pinos, and remained there until December 9th, seek-ing in vain for the harbor of Monterey, which Viz-cayno had described. On December 9th, weary, sick and disheartened, they prepared to return to San Diego, having erected on the south side of Point Pinos a large wooden cross bearing the following inscrip-tion: "Dig at the foot of this and you will find a writing." At its **foot** they buried a brief account of their **journey.**

Father Crespi made a copy of the manuscript in his diary, as follows:

"The overland **expedition, which left** San Diego **on the** 14th **of July, under the** command of Don Gaspar Portolá, Governor of California, **reached** the channel **of Santa** Barbara **on the 9th of August, and passed Point Concepcion on the 27th of the same month. It arrived at the Sierra de Santa Lucia on the 13th of September, entered** that range of mountains on **the** 17th **of the** same month, and **emerged from it on the 11th of** October; on the same **day caught** sight **of Point Pinos** and the **harbors on its north and south sides, without discovering any indications or** landmarks **of the bay of Monterey; determined to** push **on** further **in search of it, on** the **30th of** October **got** sight **of Point Reyes** and the Farallones, **off the** bay of San Francisco, **which are seven in number. The** expedition strove **to reach Point Reyes,** but was **hindered by an** immense **arm of** the sea, which, **extending to a great** distance inland, **compelled** them **to make an enormous circuit for** that purpose. **In consequence of this and other** difficulties, **the greatest of all being the absolute** want of food, the expedition **was compelled to turn back,** believing that **they must have passed the harbor of** Monterey **without** discovering **it; started on** return from the bay of San Francisco on the 11th of November; **passed Point Año Nuevo on** the 19th, **and** reached

1*

this point and harbor of Pinos on the 27th of the same month. From that date until the present, 9th of December, we have used every effort to find the bay of Monterey, searching the coast, notwithstanding its ruggedness, far and wide; but in vain. At last, undeceived, and despairing of finding it after so many efforts, sufferings and labor, and having left, of all our provisions, but fourteen small sacks of flour, we leave this place to-day for San Diego. I beg of Almighty God to guide us, and for you, traveller, who may read this, that He may guide you also to the harbor of eternal salvation.

" Done in this harbor of Pinos, the 9th of December, 1769.

" NOTE.—That Don Michael Constanzo, the engineer, observed the latitude of various places on the coast, and the same are as follows:

" San Diego, at the camp occupied by the overland expedition, 32° 42'.

" The Indian Village, at the east end of the channel of Santa Barbara, 34° 13'.

" Point Concepcion, 34° 30'.

" The southern foot of the Sierra de Santa Lucia, 35° 45'.

" The northern extremity in this harbor and Point Pinos, 36° 36'.

" Point Año Nuevo, which has low reefs of rocks, 36° 04'.

" The land near the harbor of San Francisco, having the Farallones on the west, quartering north, 37° 35'.

"Point Reyes, which we discovered on the west, northeast from the same place, supposed to be 37° 44'.

"If the commanders of the schooners, either the *San José* or the *Principe*, should reach this place within a few days after date, on learning the contents of this writing and of the distressed condition of this expedition, we beseech them to follow the coast down closely towards San Diego, so that if we should be happy enough to catch sight of them we may be able to apprise them, by signals, flags and firearms, of the place in which succor and provisions may reach us."

"Glory be to God," he adds, "the cross was erected on a little hillock close to the beach of the small harbor on the south side of Point Pinos, and at its foot we buried the letter."

Another cross was erected on the opposite side of the Point, with the inscription: "The overland expedition from San Diego returned from this place on the 9th of December, 1769, starving."

But the schooners never brought any succor to the expedition; for, after beating up to the latitude of Monterey, they were compelled to return to Santa Barbara for water, and indeed only arrived at San Diego in time to relieve the distress of the inhabitants, who were almost starving. The expedition, after encountering almost incredible hardships and losing many of its number, at last reached San Diego, the port they had started from months before.

They found that the provisions on hand were sufficient only for two or three weeks at the furthest, and the settlement was wholly dependent on the arrival of a vessel, which was expected from the coast of New Spain with provisions. The Governor, believing that the vessel had foundered, as she was out more than double the time usually consumed during the passage, declared that unless she appeared by the 20th of March, the Feast of St. Joseph, he would abandon the country and return to Old California. The missionaries were very reluctant to depart, and prayed earnestly that the long-looked for vessel might be guided safely to port. On the nineteenth of March the *San Antonio* hove in sight, with a large cargo of provisions. Arrangements were made immediately for a new expedition to the port of Monterey. Like the former one it was divided into two parts, one to proceed by sea and the other by land. They started about the middle of April, and arrived at their destination late in May.

Father Junipero Serra writes about the expedition as follows to his friend, Father Palou:

"My Dearest Friend:—On the thirty-first day of May, by the favor of God, after rather a painful voyage of a month and a half, the packet *San Antonio*, commanded by Don Juan Perez, arrived and anchored in this port of Monterey, which is unaltered in any degree from what it was when visited by the expedition of Don Sebastian Vizcayno, in the year 1602. It gave me great consolation to find that the land expedition had arrived eight days before us, and that Father Crespi and all the others were in good health. On the third of June, being the Holy Day of Pentecost, all the naval and military officers and the people assembled on a bank at the foot of an oak, where we

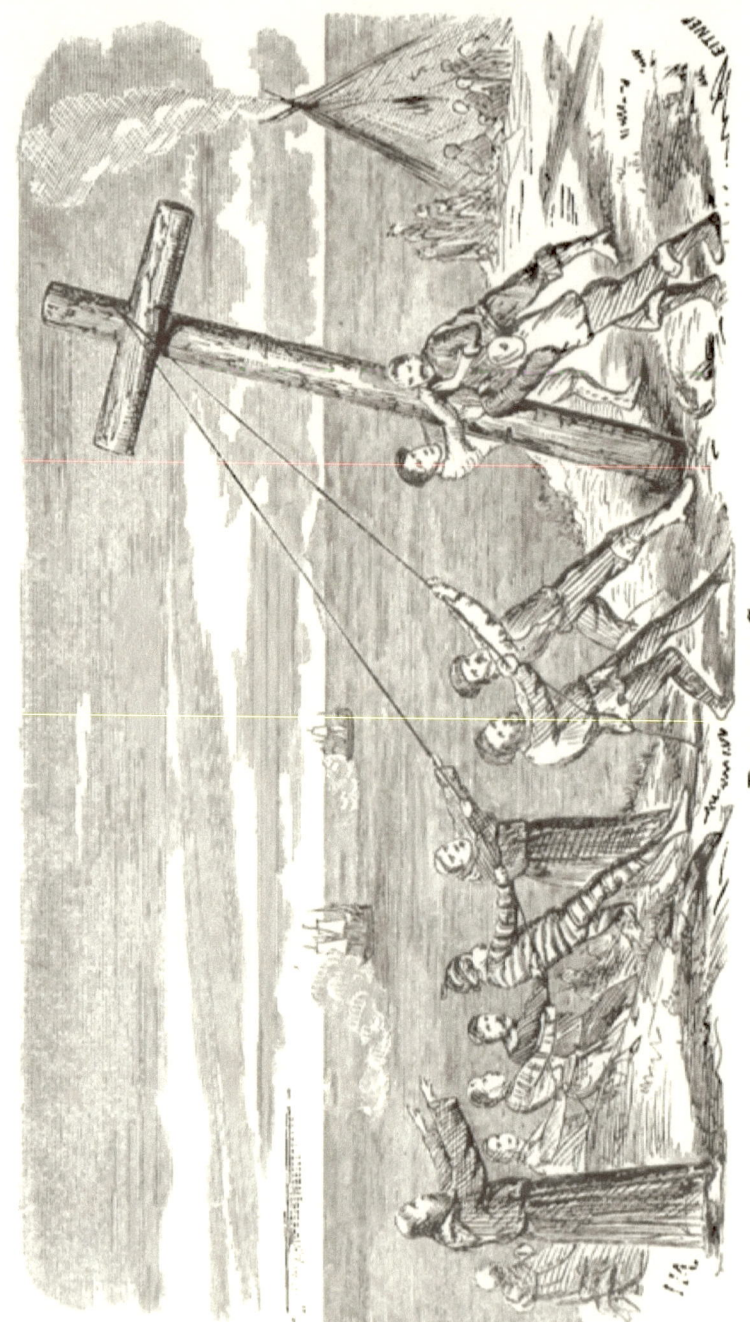

RAISING THE CROSS.

caused an altar to be erected and the bells to be rung.
We then chanted the *Veni Creator*, blessed the water,
erected and blessed a grand cross, hoisted the royal
standard and sang the first mass that ever was celebrated in this place. We afterwards sang the *Salve
Regina* before an image of the Virgin, and concluded
the whole with a *Te Deum*. After this the officers
took possession of the country in the name of the
King. We then all dined together in a shady place
on the beach," etc.

The volleys of musketry which celebrated the
establishment of the Mission so alarmed the Indians
that they withdrew and hid themselves in the mountains. After several months Father Serra began to
make converts, and on December 26th the first solemn
baptism was performed at the Mission of Monterey.

Father Serra, after an examination of the country
in the vicinity of the port, forwarded an account of
his explorations to Mexico, and demanded from the
ecclesiastical authorities an additional force of clergy.
Thirty religious embarked at San Blas in the *San Antonio* and *San Carlos*, in January and February, 1771.
When they arrived at Monterey, Father Serra offered
up a solemn High Mass in gratitude to God for this
fortunate assistance in the work of planting the Cross.
The next Mission established by Father Serra was
dedicated to Saint Antony of Padua, in the mountains
of Santa Lucia. On his return to Monterey the
Father changed the site of the San Carlos Mission.
He sent orders to Fathers Cambon and Somera to
establish a Mission to the north of San Diego, and

name it in honor of San Gabriel. Those religious
were threatened by the Indians; but, on exhibiting a
banner with the image of Our Lady of Dolores upon
it, the savages subsided and threw away their arms.
The following letter written by Father Serra will explain the progress the Missions had made at that
date:

"MISSION OF SAN CARLOS, MONTEREY,
"August 18, 1772.

"DEAR FRIEND:—Thanks be to God, I am in good
health, and suffer little from want. There is no fear
of being obliged to abandon any of the Missions now
established. The milk of the cows and the garden
vegetables have been the great sources of subsistence.
These, however, now begin to grow scarce. But of
this I do not complain, but rather that we have not
been able to go on with new Missions. All of us feel
the vexatious troubles and obstacles which we have to
encounter, yet no one thinks of leaving the Mission.
Our greatest consolation is the knowledge that from
Monterey, San Antonio and San Diego, there are
numerous souls in heaven. From San Gabriel there
are none yet; but among those Indians there are many
who praise God, and His holy name is in their
mouths more frequently than in those of many old
Christians. There are, however, those who think that
from lambs they will become tigers. This may be so,
if God permits it; but after three years' experience
with those of Monterey and two with those of San
Antonio, they appear better every day. If all are not

already Christians, it is, in my opinion, only owing to our unacquaintance with the language. This is a trouble which is not new to me, and I have always imagined that my sins have not permitted me to possess this faculty of learning strange tongues, which is a great misfortune in a country like this, where no interpreter or master of languages can be had until some of the natives learn Spanish, which requires a long time. At San Diego they have already overcome this difficulty. They now baptize adults and celebrate marriages, and we are here approximating to the same point. We have begun to explain to the youth in Spanish; and if they could return us a little assistance in another way, we should in a short time care little about the arrival of the vessels, so far as respects provisions. But, as affairs stand at present, the impious cannot much advance. Upon the whole I confide in God, who must remedy all."

He then goes on to solicit an additional number of missionaries, and concludes by saying:

"Let those who come here come well provided with patience and charity, and let them possess good humor, for they may become rich—I mean, in troubles; but where will the laboring ox go when he must not draw the plough? and if he do not draw the plough how can there be a harvest? May God preserve you for many years in His love and grace."

The first religious that suffered martyrdom was Father Luis Jayme. On the 4th of November, 1775, one thousand or more Indians assembled outside the church of San Carlos, and there divided into two bodies, one for the destruction of the Presidio and the other of the church. Father Luis, being awakened by the tumult, rushed out to appease the mob, saying "*Amar á Dios, hijos!*" (" Love God, my children.") They fell upon him with arrows, clubs and stones, and literally tore his body to pieces. A carpenter and a blacksmith, two of the Father's employés, were also killed. The attack on the soldiers was gallantly resisted, for, though turned out of the barracks, they entrenched themselves in a small hut, which they maintained until morning, when the mob dispersed. The remains of Father Luis were interred in the little chapel at the Presidio. Father Serra dispatched to Mexico, by the hands of Rivera, the Commander of Monterey, a requisition for an increase of the force of guards at the Missions. Rivera was joined at San Gabriel by an expedition commanded by Anza on its way from Sonora to the port of San Francisco. As soon as the Viceroy, Bucarelli, heard of the outrage, he wrote to Father Serra, as follows:

"I cannot express to your Reverence the sentiments with which the unhappy occurrence at the Mission of San Diego and the tragic death of Father Luis Jayme, an account of which I have received from the Commandant, Don Rivera y Moncada, and Don Bautista Anza, have inspired me. In all likelihood they would have been greater only for the opportune arrival of the last-named, with the families destined for Monterey. The arrangements which these officers have made for the security of San Diego, as well as for that of San Gabriel and San Luis, are prudent,

MARTYRDOM OF FATHER LUIS JAYME.

and such as were dictated in view of the subsequent dangers. They have informed me of the apprehension of some of the malefactors, and encourage me to look for a return of tranquillity with the punishment of the guilty. I hope for the same; but as this attempt shows me how little is to be trusted either to the neophytes or the gentiles, I have given orders to Don Rieva, Governor of the Peninsula, to recruit, if possible, twenty-five men as a reinforcement demanded by Don Rivera. The arrival of the packet boats, the *Principe* and *San Carlos,* which left for their destination on the 10th current, will serve not a little to tranquillize the inhabitants, at the same time that they will facilitate the occupation of the port of San Francisco; and as there are some on board in the capacity of soldiers, I have ordered that they should remain at San Diego. Moreover, I have ordered the Commissary at San Blas to raise some recruits without delay, and to forward them, with arms and ammunition, to the Governor. I am not unmindful of the other things to which I will give effect as soon as an opportunity occurs; and I think that, having offered this tribulation to God, you will not alter in anything your apostolic zeal, but rather trust to seeing ameliorated the constitution of these establishments, to which no doubt your Reverence will contribute much by animating the Fathers to confidence, on account of the presence of the troops."

Before proceeding to the narrative of the formal founding of the Mission of San Francisco, a brief sketch of the general plan of the Missions may prove interesting.

In 1839 the entire population of Upper California, white and mixed, was only five thousand. De Mofras, the French traveller, who visited California between the years 1841 and 1842, gives the following description of the Mission establishments at that time:

" The Mission buildings are made of adobe,* and, as at the best Mission, that of San Luis Rey, were built about a square measuring nearly 150 yards each way. The Church, which is the main part of the structure, has a portico in front. The other buildings occupying the remainder of the square, are but one-story high, and the floors (of dirt or brick) are raised a little above the level of the earth outside. The court inside the square is ornamented with fountains and trees. The small squares are occupied as lodging-places for the Fathers, mayor domos and travellers, and as workshops, schools and storehouses. The infirmaries for men and women are situated in the most quiet part of the Mission, where also are the schools. The young Indian girls dwell in a house called the convent, and they themselves are styled nuns. The Fathers are compelled to keep them closed, to protect them from the brutality of the male Indians. Placed under the care of trustworthy Indian matrons, the girls learn to weave wool, hemp and cotton ; and they never leave the convent until old enough to get married. * * *

* The Mission Churches of San Diego, Santa Barbara and San Carlos (Monterey), were built of stone.

"The reverend fathers encouraged the Indians to labor by often putting their hands to the work and always giving the example. * * * * Necessity rendered them industrious; and it is astonishing how, with so few resources—often without European laborers, assisted only by savages, almost devoid of intelligence, and often hostile—they have been able to cultivate large tracts of land, and at the same time erect spacious houses and mills, build roads, bridges and irrigating canals, and perform much mechanical labor. The timber used in the Mission buildings was usually cut on steep mountains, eight or ten leagues distant, and the Indians were taught to burn lime, cut stone and mould brick. Around the Mission square stand the workhouses, the cabins of the neophytes and the houses of the white colonists. In addition to the Mission establishments, there are fifteen or twenty accessory farms and some branch chapels within a square of thirty or forty leagues. In front of the churches is a guard-house, occupied by four horse-soldiers and a sergeant, who serve to escort the Fathers, carry despatches and help to repel the attacks of the savage tribes which in early times occasionally assailed the Missions." * * *

The daily routine at each of the establishments, according to Rev. William Gleeson's "History of the Catholic Church in California," was founded on the Jesuits' system in Lower California. At sunrise they arose and proceeded to the church where,

after morning prayers, they assisted at the holy
Sacrifice of the Mass. Breakfast next followed, when
they proceeded to their respective employments.
Towards noon they returned to the Mission and spent
the time from then till 2 o'clock, between dinner
and repose, after which they again repaired to their
work and remained engaged till the evening Angelus,
about an hour before sunset. All then betook
themselves to the church for evening devotions, which
consisted of the ordinary family prayers and the
Rosary, except on special occasions, when other devo-
tional exercises were added. After supper, which
immediately followed, they amused themselves in
divers sports, games and dancing till the hour for repose Their diet, of which the poor of any country
might be justly envious, consisted of an abundance
of excellent beef and mutton, with vegetables in the
season.   Wheaten cakes and puddings, or porridge,
called *atole* and *pinole*, also formed a portion of the
repast. The dress was, for the males, linen shirts,
trousers, and a blanket to be used as an overcoat. The
women received each, annually, two undergarments,
a gown and a blanket. In years of plenty, when the
Missions had become rich, the Fathers distributed all
the surplus money among the Indians in clothing and
trinkets. Such was the general character of the early
Missions established in Upper California by the dis-
ciples of St. Francis of Assis.

Speaking of the economy exercised by the Missionaries during their administration, De Mofras
says:

"One remarkable fact about the establishment of those Missions is, that they entailed no sacrifice upon the Government. When the first Missions were founded in Lower California the Viceroy gave some assistance. Philip V., during the first year of his reign, granted $13,000 to them; but, in 1735, the Jesuits, having received considerable donations, administered them so well that they not only paid the expenses of the Missions, but bought new lands."

The property of the Pious Fund (*Fondo Pio*) of California consisted (at the time De Mofras visited the Californias) of the haciendas of San Pedro, Torreon, Rincon, and Las Golondrinas, including several mines, workshops, and immense herds of cattle, and more than five hundred leagues of land in the State of Tamaulipas. This property was originally given to the Jesuit Fathers by the Márquis de Villa Fuente, Grand Chancellor of New Spain, and his wife, the Countess de las Torres, on the 7th of June, 1735. The Society was further enriched by large legacies of property near San Luis Potosi, Guanajuato, and Guadalajara.

We continue to quote from De Mofras:

" In 1827 the Mexican Government seized the sum of $78,000 in specie lying in the Mint at the Capital, which money belonged to the Jesuits', having been obtained by the sale of the hacienda Arroya Zarco. The Pious Fund was further despoiled of large tracts of land by the Congress of Jalisco; and finally President Santa Anna sold the entire fund to Messrs. Barajo and Rubio Bros.

" Under the Spanish Government the annual revenues amounted to about $50,000. Of this, $25,000
served to pay the expenses of the Fathers, fifteen
Dominicans [in Lower California], $600 each, and forty
Franciscans [in Upper California], $400 each, and the
remaining $25,000 was used to buy clothes, tools, and
ornaments for the churches. The Spanish Government paid for all the supplies furnished by the Missions to the Presidios. The agent who received this
payment bought merchandise which he sent at his own
expense to San Blas, and thence it was carried twice
a year in ships, without charge, to the various ports
of California.

" From 1811 to 1818, and from 1823 to 1831 the
Missions in California did not receive any money from
the Pious Fund, in consequence of the political
troubles then agitating Spain and Mexico. By adding
the sum of $92,000 due to the Franciscans of Upper
California, $78,000 taken out of the Mint of Mexico,
$270,000, value of supplies furnished by the Mis-
sions of Upper California to the Presidios, and the
revenues of the Pious Fund for more than ten years—
by adding all these together, is attained a total of a
million dollars, of which the Mexican Government
has despoiled the Missionary Society, in contempt of
the express intention of the testators.

" On the 25th of May, 1832, the Mexican Congress
passed a decree authorizing the Executive authorities
of the nation to farm out the haciendas of the Pious
Fund for seven years, the rent to be paid into the
National Treasury. A second decree of Congress,

under date of September 19, 1836, directed that the Pious Fund should be placed under the control of the new Bishop in California and his successors, so that those prelates might employ it for the development of the Missions, and for similar purposes, always respecting the will of the founders of the Fund.

"On the 8th of February, 1842, General Santa Anna, Provisional President, acting under his *discretionary* powers, took away the administration of the Pious Fund from the Bishop in California, notwithstanding the protest of the latter, and conferred it, by a decree of the 21st of the same month, on General Valencia, Chief of the Military Staff. The word "administration" has a very clear meaning to all who know the country. This was the last blow, previous to the final sale, struck at the system organized by the Jesuits. Let us add, nevertheless, that the few Franciscans still remaining in California continue to receive $400 annually, paid in merchandise charged at exorbitant rates.

* * * * * * *

"While the Mexican Government was taking possession of the Pious Fund and depriving the Fathers of the temporal administration of the Mission property, its agents were industriously engaged in pillaging the Missions and killing the cattle which formed their wealth. Already, in 1822, at the unfortunate epoch of the separation from Spain, some partisans of the new Government were heard to use the word ' secularization.'

" Nevertheless, the Spanish Missionaries resisted successfully until 1830; but, in 1831, the Reverend Father President, Sanchez, who had courageously opposed the invasion of the civil power, having died of grief, the majority of the Fathers, exposed to insult, determined to quit the country; and these men, who had devoted thirty or forty years of their lives to enlighten and civilize the Indians—who had induced the red men to abandon their wandering mode of life; who had created fine estates and bred immense herds of cattle; who had administered immense sums of money, amounting sometimes to $100,000—these venerable religious were seen departing from a country which they had enriched by their toil, and rendered fertile by their apostolic words, taking nothing with them save a coarse woollen dress."

The Mission of San Francisco.

June 17, 1776, the expeditions started from Monterey to found the Mission and Presidio of San Francisco. The land force arrived on the 27th, and encamped on the borders of a small lake, known as the " Laguna de los Dolores." There has been a difference of opinion regarding the location of this lagoon. Some writers contend that it was the place known, as late as 1861, as " The Willows," while others speak of the " Washerwoman's Lagoon," in the neighborhood of the Presidio, as the spot. It is scarcely probable that if the latter were chosen, the

Missionaries would return **so** far south to select the
site of their new Mission. General Vallejo gives his
own and the authority of the people of ninety years
ago that there used **to be a** pond, **or** " small lake," in
the Sans Souci **Valley,** north of the Mission **Dolores,
and immediately behind the hill** on which the Protes-
.**tant** Orphan Asylum **now** stands. It was the common
opinion, according to the General, that this was where
the expedition halted. There is, however, an *Atlas* in
the San Francisco **Odd** Fellows **Library, which** con-
tains all the surveys of the celebrated French expedi-
tion, under La Pérouse. They were made in the begin-
ning of the present century. In **the** *Atlas* in question we
find accurate maps of all the principal ports along the
Pacific coast. That of the Port of San Francisco was
made between **the** years 1785 and 1788. All lines and
indentations are carefully **drawn,** and the location
of every lagoon, **cove** and **inlet** is clearly defined.
The "Laguna **de los Dolores"** is placed **where the
western** part of Mission **Bay formed** an estuary, which
became a marsh, **or** " laguna," **when** the tides receded.
It is now nearly all filled in, and in the course of
time nothing will remain of La Pérouse's " Laguna
de los Dolores" **save the** canal that will **ebb** and flow
by the Channel street **of** the future.

According to Father Palou: **" On** the 27th day of
June the expedition **arrived in the** vicinity, and the
Commander ordered a halt on **the** margin of a lake
which **Señor** Anza named after Our Lady of los Dolores, **and** which was in **view of** the creek of los Llo-

2

ronas and the shore of the salt marsh or arm of the sea which runs to the southeast, with the intention of waiting for the ship to mark the spot for the location of the fort and Presidio, and in the interim to explore the land. On the following day the Commander gave orders for the construction of a hut covered with branches that should serve as a chapel wherein to celebrate the holy sacrifice of the Mass, (in which Mass was said for the first time on the 29th of June, the feast of Saints Peter and Paul), and wherein it should be celebrated daily until the removal of the camp to the site which it now occupies."

The natives came to see the strangers in great numbers, and made signs of peace and welcome. While awaiting the arrival of the store-ship, the explorers were engaged in cutting down timber for their houses, in order to establish a permanent settlement. The vessel did not arrive until the 18th of August, having had foul winds throughout the passage. On the 17th day of September—the festival of the Stigmata of St. Francis—formal possession was taken of the Presidio; and for the establishment of the Mission was selected the 4th of October, the Feast of the Seraphic Saint after whom the port was named. After blessing, reverencing and planting the holy cross, the first Mass was chanted, and the ceremony concluded by a *Te Deum ;* the act of possession in the name of the Sovereign was accompanied with many discharges of artillery and musketry by the naval and military forces. The harbor was afterwards surveyed by sea and land, and it was ascertained that the passage the expedition had entered by was the only outlet to the ocean. On the 8th day of November, the Mission was taken possession of with similar ceremonies, the want of music being supplied by the continual discharge of firearms.

The work that lay before the missionaries was one that required tact, patience and endurance. The aborigines were neither brave nor bold, generous nor spirited. According to Tuthill, they seem to have possessed none of the noble characteristics that, with a slight coloring of romance, make heroes of the red men of the Atlantic slopes and win for them our ready sympathy. We hear of no orators among them, no bold braves terribly resenting and contesting to the last the usurpation of the whites. They were " diggers," filthy and cowardly, succumbing without a blow to the rule of foreign masters. As if to redeem them from stolid brutality, occasional glimpses of humor may be noted, and a disposition to make fun of the missionary when his back was turned. But under the Father's eye they cowered like children on the low benches before the old-time pedagogue wielding the ferrule. ˙ Doubtless, the mild, patriarchal treatment of the good missionaries disarmed their hostility. Perhaps, had they been subject to the rough handling which the Indian tribes generally received from English settlers, they might have fired up and displayed some of the violence and savage fury that make us respect the Indians of the East and North. Or, it may be it was partly because they were treated as children that they grew into simple childish boys.

They were as contemptible physically as intellectually, and educed as little traces of a moral sense as of a reasoning faculty. To Drake's party they showed a disposition to offer sacrifices, thinking the "jolly tars" to be veritable gods. Venegas thought the Lower Californians to be the most stupid and weak, both in mind and body, of all mortals. But the settlers of Upper California, who had seen both, thought the northern natives far inferior to the southern. Humboldt considered them as low in the scale of humanity as the inhabitants of Van Dieman's Land. Though in many respects one people, the gibberish they spoke varied widely in different localities. Those of San Diego could not understand a word of the language of those sixty miles north, and only a high mountain range divided the dialects. They held that the inferior regions were once on a time married, and their children were the sand, and soil, rocks, stones, flints for their arrows, trees, herbs, grass and animals. There was a phantom, which they called Chinigchinich—an orphan from the beginning—who could see in the darkest night as clearly as at noon. This powerful being defended the good and chastised the bad; he was always and everywhere present, but hailed from the stars, as his home. Him they regarded as the creator of their race and as their great Captain. The land where they lived was the first land made. They seemed to believe that there was very little beyond it. The sea was at first but a fresh-water stream coursing around their little earth; but the fishes, putting their heads together, agreed and managed to

break a rock, **inside,** which was gall ; emptying this
into **the river, the** waters grew **a** little and swelled to
an ocean, **and the** thoughtful fishes **were** rewarded
with plenty of **room and a** wholesome **pickle to sport
in.** To **the great Captain, or god of the barbarous
name, they accredited** all **the precepts of morality that
they taught** their **children;** and **to** this command they
traced their customs **and** mode **of life. He** told them
to build a temple ; **so in every town close by** the
chief's **house was an** oval **enclosure made of the
branches of trees and** mats, **surrounded by stakes of
wood driven into the ground, which constituted** the
temple. It was a very sacred spot, within or near which
no irreverent act was ever performed, **for** the god
himself was there **in** the person **of a** cayote **skin** stuffed
with feathers, **claws,** talons **and beaks, which doubtless sym**bolized **the strength, swiftness and power of**
the birds and **beasts from which** they **were taken.
They worshipped** him **with** grotesque **dances and
hideous** yells, **and sometimes, in** perfect silence, squat-
ting **in most awkward attitudes in** his presence, and
retaining **one position** while **the ceremony of** adora-
tion lasted. His temple was the city of **refuge** where
the most outrageous criminal was safe, and, after **the
visit, could go free, though the crime might** be **pun-
ished on the descendants of the offender at once, or
after the lapse of generations. The boys were**
whipped **with nettles and laid upon ants' nests that**
the **stings of the insects might make them** courageous
under **the** infliction of **pain. They were** branded by
burning **moxas on the fleshy part of the arm,** to put

them above the consideration of trifling ailments. They were forbidden to warm themselves at a fire, lest they should come short of the toughness of men, and, until they were heads of families, certain food they must not touch. To violate any of these orders would let loose the evil spirit on them, and provoke the ire of the god. The girls were trained to work from infancy. At ten, to heighten their beauty, their breasts and faces were tatooed, the flesh being pricked with the thorn of the cactus until it bled, and a soft charcoal rubbed in, in lieu of India ink. On arriving at womanhood they were placed on a bed of branches, over some heated stones that were laid in a hole in the ground, and there kept, with little or no food, for three days, while ancient hags danced around the pile singing songs well calculated to inspire the wretched perspiring beauties with a sense of the vast responsibilities that pertained to their new condition. Betrothed by their parents in infancy, they were married with a good deal of ceremony, and divorced without any, at their own or their husband's will. A skin, thrown over his shoulders, constituted the full dress of a gentleman. Mats made of squirrel skins twisted into rope, sewn together, and tolerably fitted to the person, constituted a fine lady's common dress. Add a fringe of grass reaching to the knees, hang ornaments of beads and shells upon her neck, and varnish the face with colored mud, and she was dressed for a grand occasion. The San Francisco Indians are said to have used a much more simple style of dress, plastering their whole bodies with mud, especially in

the cooler months of **the year;** though, if **this were so,**
the fashion came **in** vogue probably after Drake's day,
or was **reserved for winter.** The men **made** bows and
arrows, baskets **and nets for** fishing, **killed some
small game, and fished a little when the mood was
on; but most of the work was done by the other sex.
The women went to the** woods, **gathered the** acorns
that were a staple **of** food, picked **the berries,** dug
the edible roots, gathered the firewood, **cooked,** kept
house and cared **for the** children. The **acorns** they
mashed, wet up with **water into a dough, and cooked
between hot stones. Buckeyes they rubbed down
with** water into **a thin gruel, and boiled by** throwing
hot stones into **the** mess. They held **it a** godsend
when **a** whale was stranded **on** the **coast; it** relieved
them **from the necessity of** work **for weeks,** for, **like
most gourmands who** prefer **their game a little high,
they thought the blubber improved by moderate age.**

Dancing **was a very important part of all their**
entertainments **and their religious** rites. **Save at a**
few special feasts, **the dances were** generally very
modest, the sexes dancing **apart from each** other,
though in the same room. Their god **was** a great
admirer of vigorous dancing, so dancing **was a** virtue,
and this virtue at least **was popular. War was never
their passion; but if one of a tribe stole a squirrel or
an** ornament from **another tribe, they** generally
indorsed **his theft** and maintained their **honor with**
their **arms. The war** being **ended,** the thief was dealt
with as **he deserved.** Yet it **appears that they lived**
very peacefully most of the **time, and did very little**

quarreling. On occasion of their grand feasts, scalps taken in battle were exhibited on a pole planted on a temple. The women and children who were captured in war generally stayed with their captors for life. Every town had its chief, but he enjoyed very little consideration in the town councils. If he transgressed his authority, they deposed him. His person was held in veneration, although his advice might be treated with sovereign contempt. Their medical practice was exceedingly simple. Herbs crushed or bruised and applied as a poultice was the treatment for most external diseases. For slight internal ailments they smoked the same herbs, or whipped the part affected with nettles. For serious diseases, the cold water bath was a common remedy ; that failing, the patient was laid upon the dry sand or ashes and a fire kindled at his feet, which was kept blazing night and day. Near his head was placed a cup of water or some gruel. His friends then sat down by his side and waited in patience until he recovered or died. Of course they had their quacks, who performed wonderful cures, through the medium of a perfect faith and the entire control of the patient's imagination. When one died he was either buried or burned, according as the custom of the locality was. When burning was the fashion, the corpse was laid upon a pile of faggots in the presence of the friends, and the bows and arrows, and whatever the deceased cherished as his property, were laid beside him. When the professional burners announced that all was consumed, the friends retired outside the town to do their mourning, the doctor

AN OLD MISSION CHURCH.

accompanying them and chanting the story of the fatal sickness, **while they** wept. **After three days and** nights they returned home, and cut their hair in token **of their loss. If the departed were a distant** relative **the rule required that it be cut half its old** length **; if it were a parent, wife or child, the head must be shaved close.** They thought Death was a **being who** took away a person's breath, and after that there was no more of him forever. The punishments that they **feared from** their **god were almost** entirely physical, **and pertained to this life. Still they** thought **that the heart of a good chief went up after death among the stars to** enlighten the **earth; hence, that the** stars, comets and meteors were the **hearts** of great Indians departed. Common men had no such honor awaiting them, **and the chiefs** only attained it by virtue **of the** fact that, after **death,** and before being burn**ed, men** who practiced a modified cannibalism **as** a profession **came and** with much ceremony consumed a small por-**tion of** their flesh.

The Santa Cruz Mission.

MISSION DOLORES numbered already **fifteen years of existence, and** hundreds of neophytes **had** gathered beneath **the shadow of** its Cross, while **the** benighted Indians **around** Aptos and **Santa Cruz were** still buried in the darkness of paganism.

* 2

Strange to say, before the expedition by land, accompanied by Fathers Crespi and Gomez, had discovered the magnificent Bay of San Francisco, it had already reposed under one of the mammoth redwood trees which then crowned the adjacent mountains and hills, even to the very shores of the Pacific, or lain down under the canopy of heaven on a soft bed of grass, gemmed with fragrant wild roses, along the banks of the San Lorenzo, where now shines in beauty the City of the Holy Cross.

Why the foundation of this Mission was so long postponed, we cannot ascertain; but we may surmise one of the causes to be that, when the first expedition passed through, no Indians appeared around the place; and though in subsequent expeditions Father Palou descried a few of the native race peeping timidly from behind the trees, the explorers may have deemed that there was not a sufficient number to justify the establishment of a Mission.

The old records of Santa Cruz tell us that the Mission Indians were never numerous there, and did not number more than three or four hundred, while in other Missions they were counted by thousands.

The day of grace, however, dawned finally for those children of the woods. In a record of that parish we read that on the 25th of September, 1791, Fathers Alonzo Salazar and Baldomeros Lopez planted the Mission Cross there for the first time.

They lived for awhile in huts constructed of branches of trees, covered with mud ; a provisional church was also erected. The first stone of the adobe structure, now in ruins, was laid with **great** solemnity, on **the 27th of February,** 1793, the **soldiers, Indians and** officiating priests being present. It was completed on **the 10th of May,** 1794, **and** was dedicated with **the usual ceremonies,** Father **Tómas Peña** (missionary **of Santa Clara,) the** commanding officer **of the Presidio of San Francisco** (Hermenegildo Sal,) besides **four other** priests, assisting on **the** occasion. The walls were built very thick (nearly five feet); the length of the **church** was **112½ feet, 29 feet** wide, **and** 25½ **feet in height.**

Nearly all the adobe churches of California were **very long and narrow. Among those yet** standing which have seen their first centenary, are that **of** San Luis Obispo, **built** August 19th, **1772, and** that of Monterey, **built June 3d, 1770. But** the **Mission** church **of Santa Cruz has not been** destined **to behold its** first **centennial. It had scarcely** fifty **years of existence when part of it fell down. It was repaired; but a few** years **after (in 1857) the front walls** fell in. On account **of threatening danger it had finally** to be demolished, **and** of **the** old **church nothing** now remains save the side walls of the sanctuary, **the** vestry, **and a long building in the rear** which **is** used for storage. It is now covered with a new roof of shingles, and its present existence **is probably due to the strong iron braces** that **support it.**

It was customary for one Mission **always to receive** assistance **from the** others at their **foundation.** Father Olber tells **us that "at** the foundation **of the** Mission of Santa **Cruz, Santa Clara gave to us thirty** cows, five yoke of oxen (two pair very bad), fourteen bulls, twenty steers, and nine horses." The Mission of Carmelo gave seven mules. According to Father Olber, the Mission of San Francisco showed a questionable generosity, for the old missionary, in a quiet humor, observes that " of the five yoke of oxen which the Mission of our Father Saint Francis gave us, we had to kill a pair, *so bad were they;* and of the seven mules received from Carmel, one was so *gentle* that he died three days after." However, he acknowledges to having received from San Francisco " sixty sheep, ten rams, and two bushels of barley."

Their pecuniary resources seem to have been limited in the beginning. Father Olber says that in a few days " they ran short of provisions, and had to apply to the soldiers, who assisted them with beans, corn and chocolate, to the amount of $42," which value, the Father does not fail to assure us, was returned to them afterwards.

From 1791 to 1814 there were 1,684 baptisms, 565 marriages, 1,242 deaths, and the number of Indians then living at the Mission was 388, which can be safely taken as a fair average of the past years. The cattle had increased to 3,300 head; sheep to 3,500; horses to 600; mules to 25; hogs to 46. In the year 1814, forty-five bushels of wheat, seven bushels of barley, six bushels of peas, one bushel of corn, and one bushel of beans were sown; and 500 bushels of wheat, 200 of barley, 200 of peas, and 189 of corn was the product of the harvest of that year. In 1834, when the Mission was secularized, the cattle were valued at

RUINS OF THE MISSION OF SAN CARLOS.

$5,329, and the sheep at $2,219. In fact, the liquidated value of the entire Mission property was estimated at $97,361 96. This speaks well for the economy and industry of the good Fathers, who, in the space of forty-three years, made the Mission so prosperous that, from a very humble beginning, it raised itself to be able to maintain hundreds of Indians and give a helping hand to those colonists who established themselves in the adjacent village of Branciforte.

But if the Mission of Santa Cruz was rich in secular things, it was still richer in ornaments connected with the church. The tower had nine bells, some of which were valued at $800 each. The tower and bells together are said to have cost $3,900. The church was also very rich in vestments. A chasuble alone, still in a good state of preservation, was valued at $800. There are copes which cost $600 each. The silverware and vestments must have cost many thousands of dollars, which, together with other articles consecrated to Divine worship, were valued at $27,569! This speaks volumes in favor of the poor Franciscans who, contented with a bare subsistence, employed all their means for the benefit of their neophytes and the honor and glory of God.

A great deal more could be written about Santa Cruz; but we must pass to other Missions. Let us hope, however, that though the buildings have crumbled to dust, the fruits of the Christian civilization which was planted by the missionaries shall remain for ever; and though a few years hence not one of the old natives will be in existence—the oldest of them then living, a blind man one hundred years old, having died on the last day of 1876—still it is to be hoped that the new generation taking possession of the Indians' lands will always cherish a respect, at least, for those self-sacrificing men who, with the light of the Gospel, banished the darkness of ignorance and paganism.

What was once the Mission orchard is now cut up into building lots, and many families live there ; and the track of the Felton railroad now passes over the very spot where, in 1812, the good Father Quintana was killed by the Indians.

The Santa Cruz of to-day promises at no distant day to realize the anticipations of Father Palou. On his way to Monterey, in 1775, returning from his expedition to the Bay of San Francisco, he passed where Santa Cruz now is situated, and, looking around, he said it was a good spot, not only for a Mission, but for a town, and, even more, for a large city. The Mission came and passed away; the town succeeded the Mission; and, ere long, a city, with at least 15,000 inhabitants, will take the place of the humble village of Branciforte on one side and the unpretending town on the other side of the San Lorenzo.

The Mission of San Juan.

THE Mission of San Juan Bautista was founded in the reign of Charles IV., King of Spain, and his Excellency the Marquis de Branciforte, in a place called by the natives "Popelonichom," and, by the first explorers, "San Benito." It was begun on the feast of its patron, St. John the Baptist, June 24th, 1797, those present being the President of the Missions of New California, Father Fermin de Lazuen, Father Magin Catalá, and Father José Manuel de Martiarena. The troops destined to guard the place were present, as also many Indians, who showed themselves very much pleased with the ceremony.

The President, Father de Lazuen, blessed the waters and the place around, erected a large cross and, with befitting homage to the symbol of Redemption, sang the Litanies of the Saints, celebrated Mass, and exhorted those present to co-operate with him in the good work, concluding the whole with the *Te Deum*.

The first ministering priests were Father Manuel and Father Adriano Martinez. The first baptism took place on the 11th of July, 1797. The name of the child, when a gentile, was "Tixidies;" in baptism John the Baptist was given.

The first stone was not laid till the 13th of June, 1803, and the church was not completed till 1812. It was dedicated on the 23d of June of that year. The missionaries of San Francisco, San José and Santa Clara were present at the dedication. D. Manuel Gutierrez, a resident of Los Angeles, acted as sponsor. When the church was dedicated, the Fathers had baptized already 1963 persons, between children and adults. The buildings and church—scarcely over fifty years old—are yet in a good state of preservation.

San Juan is a very quiet place, and numbers but a few hundred inhabitants. When the stages going south used to pass through the town there lingered some animation there, and many travellers could be seen, covered with dust, making the long corridors echo to the sound of their footsteps as they tried to get a glimpse of the old Mission church which, being very long, presents a venerable aspect. But now all is silent. The railroad passes along a few miles from San Juan, and leaves it again in the partial silence and quietude of the past. It now greatly rests with the rich land-owners, who own immense tracts of land in the vicinity, whether it is not better for the future prosperity of San Juan that they should sub-divide their lands and open them up to industrious families, who will cultivate that beautiful valley and fill it with an enterprising population. Let us hope that, when the old Mission bells, from the top of their substantial new tower, will sound peals of joy announcing the centennial of the Mission, that there will throng thousands of inhabitants to hear them and join in fraternal accord to celebrate the happy era which brought, along with the Gospel of Christ, the sweet fruits of modern arts and industry.

The Mission of Santa Barbara.

WE take pleasure in presenting an extract from a letter of Very Rev. Father Gonzalez, of the Order of

SANTA BARBARA.

church at Santa Cruz, and to whom we are indebted
for many interesting items in this volume in connection
with the Mission of Santa Cruz and others of the
southern counties), written in September, 1864, from
the Apostolic College of Our Lady of Los Dolores,
Santa Barbara. Father Gonzalez was the last of the
old pioneer missionaries who labored to plant the
Cross in these golden regions. In this letter he
gives to the young missionary a general view of the
state of the Missions on his arrival in Upper California:

"REV. AND DEAR SIR:—On my landing in this country, which happened on the 15th of January, 1833,
there were in existence from San Diego up to San
Francisco Solano 21 Missions, which provided for
14,000 or 15,000 Indians. Even the poorest Missions,
that of San Rafael and Soledad, provided everything
for divine worship, and the maintenance of the Indians.
The care of the neophytes was left to the Missionary, who, not only as Pastor, instructed them in their
religion and administered the sacraments to them, but
as a householder, provided for them, governed and instructed them in their social life, procuring for them
peace and happiness.

"Every Mission, rather than a town, was a large
community, in which the Missionary was President,
distributing equally burdens and benefits. No one
worked for himself, and the products of the harvest,
cattle and industry in which they were employed was
guarded, administered and distributed by the Missionary. He was the Procurator and Defender of his
neophytes, and, at the same time, their Chief and

Justice of Peace, to settle all their quarrels, since the Mission Indians were not subject to the public authorities, except in grievous and criminal cases.

"This system, though criticized by some politicians, is the very one that made the Missions so flourishing. The richest in population was that of San Luis Rey; in temporal things, that of San Gabriel. Mine was that of San José, and, although I was promised, as it was on the gentile frontier, it would not be secularized, it, too, succumbed in 1836.

"In the inventory made in January, 1837, the result showed that said Mission numbered 1,300 neophytes, a great piece of land, well tilled; the store-houses filled with seeds ; two orchards, one with 1,600 fruit trees ; two vineyards—one with 6,039 vines, the other with 5,000; tools for husbandry in abundance; shops for carpenters, blacksmiths, shoemakers, and even tanneries, and all the implements for their work.

"The fields were covered with live stock: horned cattle, 20,000 head; sheep, 15,000; horses, 459. For the saddle 600 colts of two years, 1,630 mares, 149 yoke of oxen, 30 mules, 18 jackasses, and 77 hogs.

"Twice a year a new dress was given to the neophytes, amounting in the distribution to $6,000. When the Mission was secularized I delivered to the Mayordomo then in charge some $20,000 worth of cloth and other articles which the store-house contained.

"The church of the Mission of San José was neatly adorned, and well provided with vestments and other religious articles. Thirty musicians served in the choir, and they had a very neat dress for feast days.

"Of the Mission of Santa Clara, we can say the same more or less.

"The other Missions, called 'the Northern,' through having been already secularized, were in utter bankruptcy, and the same can be affirmed for the most part of those of the south, down to San Diego ; for it was observed that as long as the Missions were in the hands of the missionaries everything was abundant; but as soon as they passed into the hands of laymen everything went wrong, till eventually complete ruin succeeded, and all was gone. Yet, we cannot say that the ambition of those men was the cause, since, though the Government in the space of four years, divided seven ranches to private individuals—the smallest of a league and a half—yet in spite of this cutting off of part of my Mission lands, the Mission was every day progressing more and more.

"We have not to attribute the destruction of these establishments to rapacity; for though we can presume that something was taken, this was not the principal agent of destruction; but the blunder was made in their enterprises and the high fees paid to the Chief Steward and other salaried men, etc.

"The Government of Mexico, up to the year 1830, acknowledged, a debt in favor of these Missions of over $400,000, without counting other minor debts. Finally, we have to acknowledge that a manifest punishment from God was the cause of the destruction of the Missions, since theft alone could not accomplish it and the subsidy given to the Government would not affect them. On the contrary, left to the priests, the Missions would have prospered, and other establishments still more opulent would have been erected in the Tulares, even without any protection from the Government, and deprived of the subsidy of the Pious Fund of $400,000, if the revolution of Spain in the year 1808 and that of Mexico in 1810 had not put an end to the prosperity of the missionaries. If zealous missionaries had been left amongst the savage tribes roaming through this vast territory, from the Sierra Nevada to the Coast Mountains, called then by the priests ' Tulares,' all would have been converted to Christianity, and would not have perished, as we see them now.

" I was able to save only a small relic of these tribes during the pestilence of 1833, in which I collected together some 600 Indians. I would have saved more during the small-pox epidemic of 1839, but my Mission had already been secularized, and I had no resources. I could do nothing for the Indians, who were like boys of one hundred years. It is only with liberality you can draw them towards you: give them plenty to eat and clothes in abundance, and they will soon become your friends, and you can then conduct them to religion, form them to good manners, and teach them civilized habits.

" Do you want to know who were the cause of the ruin of these Missions? As I was not only a witness but a victim of the sad events which caused their destruction, I have tried rather to shut my eyes that I might not see the evil, and close my ears to prevent hearing the innumerable wrongs which these

SAN FRANCISCO SOLANO AMONG THE INDIANS.

establishments had suffered. My poor neophytes did their part, in their own way, to try and diminish my sorrow and anguish."

And here let us imitate the venerable Father Gonzalez, and close, also, our eyes; **for some of** those who enriched **themselves with the** spoils **of** the **poor Indians are still** living. May God avert from them that terrible saying of St. Peter: "Keep thy money **to** thyself to perish with thee."—Acts viii. 20.

The Pioneer Missionaries.

As his Grace, the Most Reverend Archbishop of San Francisco, has, in a memorable discourse which will be found in these pages, referred to **the** " **sad** human vicissitudes" which " determined that the sons of St. Francis, and, soon after, those of St. Dominic, should succeed to the charge of the Missions," some notice, however brief and rapidly sketched, of the labors of the Society of Jesus in Lower California may not be uninteresting in a Memoir like the present.

The introduction of Christianity into California dates **from the arri**val in St. Denis' Bay of the Rev. Father John Maria **Salva** Tierra, of the Society **of** Jesus, on the 19th **day** of October, **1697.** From the very outset Father Tierra had placed his enterprise under the protection of the Mother of God, whose help he was wont to invoke at all times with the loving hope and confidence **of** a true **child of** the Immaculate Virgin. If **the** difficulties **in his** path **were**

assuredly formidable, his fortitude was worthy of his
holy model, the Apostle of the Indies, St. Francis
Xavier. Separated for a considerable time from his
brethren of the Society, in a strange land and amid a
people prone to the darkest deeds of savagery, constantly exposed to grave perils through the unfriendly
feeling of the Spanish authorities, the illustrious pioneer missionary never succumbed, even for a moment,
to the rigors of his lot. Some idea of his sublime
·spirit in adversity may be gleaned from his remark in
a letter to a friend: "Henceforth, the standard of
Christ will not be removed from these countries, and
Mary will, undoubtedly, lay the foundation of her holy
house among the elect." Of the pioneer missionary's
auxiliaries in the spiritual conquest of California—
Fathers Kühno, Tempis, Copart, Goni, Peter and John
Ugarte, Piccolo, Bassaldua, Titlo and Rohen (martyrs),
Mayarga, Guillen, Bravo, Everard Helen, Keller,
Echiverria, Tarraval, Neumayer, Cabranco and Tama-
rál, (martyrs), Laymundo, Consag, Ketz, Sedelmayer,
and other members of the Society—representatives,
unlike their successors, the Franciscan Fathers, of
many nationalities—it is hardly necessary to speak
within the narrow limits of the present work. It is
not, however, too much to say that the Jesuit Fathers
in question furnished splendid examples of Christian
zeal and heroism to their Franciscan successors. Of
Father Kühno, a native of Trent, and in early life
Professor of Mathematics in the University of Ingols-
tadt, in Bavaria—the first associate, it should be remembered, of Father Salva Tierra in California—we

read, in the "Apostolicos Afanes de la Compañia de Jesus," that he baptized forty thousand of the aborigines, **and** reclaimed them from barbarism ! **As a champion and** protector **of** the Indians cruelly **oppressed** by the brutal terrorism of **the** Spanish **colonists, the good father emulated the zeal and** benignant **spirit of the great** Dominican, Las Casas. **In** 1698, **we are** told, Father Kühno "set **out on** a tour of inspection, and, after proceeding as **far** north as **the** Gila, turned west **till he came to the** head of the Gulf. Thence, continuing **his course to the south, on arriving at the Mission Dolores he had traveled** on **foot from nine to ten hundred miles. This, in a** country destitute of every convenience, wild, rugged and mountainous, and inhabited only by uncivilized races, was **a most arduous and** perilous **adventure.** But **it was** only **one of many a** similar **kind. During the** subsequent years **of his ministry he made other equally** lengthened, **arduous and** perilous journeys, sometimes **for** the **purpose of** preaching the Gospel, sometimes for quelling rebellion, sometimes for reconciling enemies, and sometimes **with the view of** promoting **the people's** social **condition,** by instructing **them in the means necessary** for providing **for** their temporal wants."* **To the** same eminent authority we are indebted **for the** subjoined notice **of** another Jesuit missionary: "**Father** Lestiago, who was **of Mexican** extraction, **was** born at Tepustucula, in 1684. **He** entered the Society when young,

---

* "History of the Catholic Church in California." **By W.** Gleeson, M.A.

and gained the general esteem of his companions as
well by his virtue as by his ability.   While professor
of Belles-Lettres, he was appointed to the Californian
Mission, whither he immediately repaired.   During
the twenty-nine years he lived in the country, he
propagated religion across the whole of the peninsula.
Frequently, he would rally forth into the mountains
in quest of the savages, having only for his support
a little corn in a sack.   There, deprived of the
ordinary comforts of life, he would remain preaching
and catechizing till his presence was demanded elsewhere.   What he suffered on those occasions, having
to accommodate himself to the barbarous life of the
people—exposed to the inclemency of the season—
can be hardly conceived.   It was thus he learned
to dispense with the use of a bed (a luxury he never
allowed himself towards the end of his days,) for
having to lead the same life as the people, he was
obliged to sleep on the ground.   He always slept
in his clothes, and rose ordinarily *two hours before day*,
in order to occupy himself in prayer and preparation
for the holy sacrifice of the Mass.   At times, while
making excursions through the woods in company
with his neophytes, he would cry out in a transport
of zeal: ' Come—oh! come all to the faith of Jesus
Christ ; oh! who will make them all Christians, and
conduct them to Heaven!'   So little was his heart
attached to temporal things, that on one occasion,
when his people presented him with some pearls they
had picked up on the shore after a storm, he ordered
them to go and throw them back into the sea!''   Of

HISTORIC OUTLINES. **49**

Father Neumayer, we are informed by the Rev.
Father Gleeson, that his career in California extended
over a period of twenty years, during which, like his
brethren, he was remarkable for great zeal and holiness of life. His character seems to have been to
accommodate himself to every circumstance, the better
to gain the affections of all, and thereby promote
more securely, the interest of his heavenly Master.
In the fields, he labored in company with the culti-
vators of the soil. On sea, he took his net and
assisted the fishermen. At home, he was an architect,
a carpenter, a blacksmith, or whatever else the circumstances demanded. The wonderful providence
of God, which overruleth and disposeth all things
according to appointment, never failed to provide for
the pressing wants of the Missions. Whenever
death removed any of the Fathers, others were found
ready to step into their place. Two months before
the death of the above-mentioned Father, two other
Religious, Fathers Franco and Ames, arrived in the
country.

Those who know anything of the self-sacrificing
spirit that has always animated the Society of Jesus
will not be surprised to learn that the Provincial of
the Society in Mexico—Father Francis Cevallas—
" offered the Viceroy to renounce all the Californian
Missions, and those of New Spain, in order that the
missionaries might be employed to greater advantage
among the gentiles of the North." And here it should
not be forgotten that from the very first, Fathers
Kühno and Salva Tierra had cherished the hope of

3

reclaiming from paganism and idolatry the inhabitants from Mexico to Oregon—an enterprise which would, in all probability, have been crowned with success under a more generous dispensation at Madrid. Although the offer of retiring from California in quest of new fields of missionary effort in the North was not accepted, through the advice of the Mexican hierarchy, the self-denial of the Society was manifest in the rejection by the Fathers of property amounting to upwards of half a million of dollars donated by a Mexican lady for missionary purposes in California.

Through the zeal and untiring labors of the Jesuit Fathers during a period of seventy years, the symbol of salvation had been planted from Cape San Lucas to the mouth of the Colorado. They were the earliest explorers of the barbarous solitude of the magnificent Empire of Spain in the New World. Traces of their benignant sway may yet be found from the highlands of New Mexico to the arid jungles of Arizona. For two hundred years the GREAT ORDER, as Lord Macaulay styles the Company of St. Ignatius, had vindicated the glory of the Catholic name in the Old World and the New. True to the imperishable principle of their institute—"*Ad Majorem Dei Gloriam*"— the sons of Loyola had been the chief champions of the Cross in every region of the earth. In all the countries of Europe, when the Reformation (so-called) threatened to submerge the very landmarks of loyalty to the Apostolic See and to sweep away "the fair humanities of old Religion," the Society of Jesus,

then in its first growth, and whose members were the-
ologians-elect to the Vicar of Christ, constituted the
bulwark of the Catholic war. In India, China, North,
South and Central America, its services were not less
memorable. Nor, amid trophies so radiant, and so
splendid an accumulation of renown, is it the least
glory of the Great Order that, at its suppression, in
1773—a measure conceived in a Satanic spirit by the
infidel Governments of France, Spain and Naples—
strong in its own innocence, in the number of its
children, and in the love of all Catholics worthy of the
name—it submitted to the authority of the Church
" without a murmur, a reproof or a complaint." Of
the persecution of the Society of Jesus in the Spanish
Monarchy and its colonial dependencies, Father Gleeson thus writes: "On the 2d of April, 1767, all the
Jesuits throughout the whole of the Spanish dominions,
both at home and abroad, in the East and the
West, were seized by order of Charles III, and without any hearing or trial, without even knowing the
cause of complaint, were thrown into prison, and
treated as the veriest criminals. The numbers sub-
jected to this horrible outrage, unparalleled in the annals of history, amounted in all to close on six thous-
and. On the same 2d of April, his Majesty issued a
royal proclamation, or pragmatic sanction, in order
to justify himself in the eyes of his subjects, declaring
that the motives which urged him to that course were
sufficient, but yet should *ever remain buried in his
royal breast*, and that if he did not act with greater severity, it was only owing to *clemency*. The document

also made known to the public that any one convicted of speaking or writing in favor of the Fathers would be considered guilty of a capital offence. Even parents were strictly prohibited holding intercourse, directly or indirectly, with their children of the Society. Tyranny, absurdity and folly could hardly proceed to further extremes." We cannot resist the pleasure of giving Father Gleeson's statement *in extenso:*

"In California, the royal instructions were carried out with the same vigor and promptitude as in the other dependencies, with this only difference, that the distance from Spain prevented their being executed on the day appointed by the king. Their execution was entrusted to Don Gaspar Portolá, who was named Governor of the country. He was attended by a body of troops, fifty in number, in order that, if necessary, he might be able to forcibly expel the Religious. The Governor and party arrived in the country toward the end of November, 1767, and immediately proceeded to execute the royal commands. Up to this moment the Fathers were entirely unaware of what was about to take place. They had not heard of the proceedings in Europe and Mexico. In compliance with an invitation of the Governor, to meet him at Loretto, the Father Visitor arrived there on the eve of the Nativity of Our Blessed Redeemer. On the following day, which should have been one of rejoicing rather than of mourning, he heard from the lips of the Governor the contents of the fatal decree. It was read for him and his companions, in the presence of the necessary witnesses. From that moment they were no longer their own masters; they were prisoners in the hands of the civil authorities. If they were not cast into prison, it was merely owing to the kindness and humanity of the Governor. They were, however, obliged to hand over all charge of their establishments, and to give an account of all their possessions; while, at the same time, they found themselves prohibited from exercising any public ecclesiastical functions. Thereupon, the Superior immediately wrote to all the Religious,

acquainting them with the unpleasant instructions of government. It was a part of the Governor's order that they were to
remain at their several posts till replaced by the expected Franciscans, then on their way to the country, when they should
repair to Loretto, bringing with them only the most necessary
articles. The instructions of the Governor also required them to
preach to their flocks, exhorting them to obedience and submission to the new order of things. Having faithfully executed
the orders of their Superior, the Fathers started for Loretto.
The scene witnessed through the country, as they parted with
their respective congregations, has never been equalled in the
history of California. The loss of friends, relatives or parents
could not evoke a greater expression of grief and affection. The
remembrance of all that the Fathers had done for them, the
blessings, spiritual and temporal, which they had conferred on
them, now came strongly before the minds of the people, and
produced the liveliest sentiments of sorrow and gratitude.
Others, indeed, it is true, were coming to replace them, but they
were strangers, and unacquainted with the language and manners of the people. At length the fatal moment arrived. On the
same day, and about the same hour, all the Religious, except
those of Loretto, bid a farewell adieu to their respective people.
The impression made on the natives is best described in the
words of one who took part in one of those scenes: 'The fatal
day is come. All the people surround the altar in silence, to
assist at the holy Sacrifice for the last time. The mass finished,
the Father proceeds to the door to take a last farewell of his
desolate children. At that moment all threw themselves upon
him, kissing his hands and sobbing aloud, pressing him, at the
same time, with such fervor, that he was well-nigh being
smothered. On the other hand, the pastor gave expression to
his grief in an abundance of tears, and knew not how to disen-
gage himself from the arms of the people.' Thus, with hearts
full of grief and eyes streaming with tears, these simple-minded,
affectionate people parted with their Fathers, their guides and
support. In other instances, their affection was expressed more
convincingly. The pastor of the Mission of St. Gertrude, the

Rev. Father Retz, being unable to walk or to ride, on account of an accident he had met with a little before, the Christians, in order that he might not be disappointed in joining his brethren, bore him on their shoulders a distance of one hundred and twenty miles to the Mission of Loretto.

"Arrived at that place, the Fathers lost no time in taking their departure. There were, in all, fifteen and a lay-brother, the exact number of those who had died in the country. The 3d of February was fixed for their departure; but the Governor, fearing the impression that their departure might make on the people if conducted by day, ordered the embarkation to take place in the night. The precaution, however, was unavailing, for no sooner were they taken out than the whole town was astir. The simple announcement, ' The Fathers are going,' drew every one that was capable of moving to the spot. In vain would the soldiers endeavor to keep them at a distance. With a common impulse, caused by love and grief, and which brooks neither delay nor hindrance, the entire multitude prostrated themselves on the ground before the assembled Religious, some giving expression to their sorrow and affection by kissing their hands and feet, others on their knees imploring pardon for their past offences; while others, still more ardent in their affection, pressed the Fathers tenderly in their arms as they wished them a lasting and parting adieu. This painful spectacle at an end, the missionaries addressed their last words to the people. They were short but impressive: 'Adieu, dear Indians; adieu California; adieu, land of our adoption: *fiat voluntas Dei.*' Then, amid the tears, the sobs and lamentations of the multitude, the fifteen Jesuit Fathers, reciting aloud the Litany of the Blessed Mother of God, turned their face from the land of their labors, banished by orders of a monarch whose only reason for expelling them from his dominions were the imaginary crimes laid to their charge by the enemies of religion. Thus, on the 3d of February, 1768, were lost to California the presence and labors of that noble and devoted body of men, who, during the comparatively short period of their missionary career, had converted the whole of Lower California from Cape San Lucas to the mouth of the Colorado."

THE COMMEMORATION.

The Centennial Celebration, on Sunday, October 8th, 1876, may be truly described as a memorable event in the annals of the commercial metropolis of California. It was, indeed, fitting that the one hundredth anniversary of San Francisco should awaken solemn memories, mellowed by sympathy for the departed soldiers of the Cross who had, despite many obstacles, vindicated the glory of their Seraphic founder and the self-denying purity of their Order on the shores of the Pacific:

> "Who hath not shared that calm so still and deep—
> The voiceless thought that would not speak but weep—
> A holy concord and a bright regret,
> A glorious sympathy with suns that set:
> 'Tis not harsh sorrow, but a tenderer woe,
> Nameless but dear to gentle hearts below,
> Felt without bitterness, but full and clear,
> A sweet dejection, a transparent tear,
> Unmixed with worldly grief, or selfish stain,
> Shed without shame, and secret without pain.
> Even as the tenderness that hour instills
> When Summer's day declines along the hills,
> So feel the fullness of our heart and eyes
> When all of goodness that can perish dies!"

Nor is it strange that orators the most distinguished should proffer their homage at the shrine of Christian heroism and self-sacrificing devotion. Already the noblest intellects of England and France, albeit not in communion with the Catholic Church, had recognized the services rendered to civilization by the Fathers of the Society of Jesus among the Indians of Paraguay; and it was happily reserved for our Centennial celebration to evoke a tribute of eloquence not less spirit-stirring and sincere. Of the discourse delivered by his Grace the Most Reverend Archbishop of San Francisco, in which, in a spirit worthy of a former era of Christian oratory, the mitred son of St. Dominic, with all the fervor and genius of the Friars Preachers, dwelt upon the labors of the children of St. Francis, it is not for us to speak; nor is it necessary to indicate at length our admiration for the orations of Hon. John W. Dwinelle and Gen. M. G. Vallejo, the representatives on the occasion of the Anglo-Saxon and Iberian races. The martial pageantry, apart from the magnificent civic demonstration, and, above all, the religious ceremonies—supreme, it need scarcely be said, in grandeur, and breathing, amid soul-thrilling strains and clouds of incense, with a sublime significance and a solemn purpose—was not the least splendid feature of the event. If, indeed, some nationalities in our cosmopolitan city were unhappily absent from the array, the blood of America, Spain and Ireland was worthily represented. In the same ranks marched shoulder to shoulder the descendants of the Conquistadores of

Old Spain, the Pioneers of the Eastern States, and the sons of the Catholic Island of the West ; and for the first time since O'Neil, O'Donnell, Blake, O'Reilly, O'Donoju—the last Viceroy of the Spanish crown in the New World—and unconquered Wellington, led, as Captains-General, the forces of Spain on many a field of fame, soldiers of Spanish blood were mustered under the bâton of an Irish Grand Marshal.

It is not too much to say that, viewed in every aspect, that celebration of the Founding of the Presidio of San Francisco and the Mission Dolóres was not unworthy of the event which' it commemorated. Although the dawn was overcast and broke over the green hills somewhat inauspiciously—spiritualizing, mayhap, the ordinarily bright skies of our favored clime—the *genius loci* seemed, as it were, to shine through the gloom, and to invest the festal occasion with a halo. At the Old Mission grounds on the corner of Sixteenth and Dolores streets, consecrated by the labors and watered by the tears of the heroic sons of St. Francis whose blood has crimsoned the sands of the Pacific, the celebration was inaugurated with a grandeur and solemnity befitting so important an anniversary. The exercises commenced with a Grand Pontifical Mass at 10 o'clock A. M., the Right Rev. Dr. O'Connell, Bishop of Marysville, officiating as celebrant. Beneath a tasteful gothic arch, adorned with ferns, ivy, clematis and wreaths of flowers and tropical plants, the temporary altar was erected. Rev. Dr. Cassidy of Mission San José officiated as Deacon, the Rev. Father Garriga as Sub-Deacon, and the

3*

Very Rev. Father Gibney, Vicar-General, as Assistant
Priest.   Within the rail presided his Grace the Most
Rev. Archbishop of San Francisco, attended by the
Rev. Fathers McSweeny and Richardson.   The Rev.
Fathers Bowman and O'Connor acted as Masters of
Ceremonies.   Among the ecclesiastics present, in
addition to the secular clergy, were representatives
of the Orders of St. Francis, St. Dominic and the
Society of Jesus: Very Rev. Father Vilarrasa, O. P.,
Rev. Father Derham, O. P., Rev. Father Harring-
ton, O. P., Rev. Father Di Marzo, O. P., Rev.
Father Callaghan, O. P., Rev. Father Alvarez, O. S. F.,
of the Franciscan College of Santa Barbara, and
Rev. Father Varsi, S. J., of Santa Clara College.   On
the right of the altar were the Grand Marshal, James
R. Kelly, and his Aids; on the left, his Excellency
William Irwin, Governor of California; Hon. A. J.
Bryant, Mayor of San Francisco; Hon. T. B. Shan-
non, Collector of the Port of San Francisco; Hon.
John M. Coghlan, United States District Attorney;
Major-General Vernon and Staff; Brigadier-General
McComb and Staff; Supervisors Macdonald, Roberts
and Hayes; City and County Attorney Burnett; School
Director Ames; the Spanish, Russian, Portuguese,
Chilean and Costa Rican Consuls; D. J. Oliver and
D. T. Murphy, Knights of the Order of St. Gregory;
as well as many prominent citizens.   Upwards of
5,000 people were present.   The choir consisted of
an orchestral band and an admirably trained male
and female chorus, under the direction of Professor
Wm. Toepke, organist of St. Mary's Cathedral; the solo

singers being Miss Kate Eishon and Mrs. R. Uhrig, sopranos; Mrs. Wm. Toepke and Mrs. O. Borreman, altos; Messrs. Bianchi and Morell, tenors; and Messrs. Borreman and Doscher, bassos. Beethoven's Mass in C was excellently rendered, as well as the Offertory *Ave Maria*, by Loretz. At the Elevation, the military presented arms amid the roll of drums and the swell of martial music. At the conclusion of the Gospel his Grace the Most Rev. Archbishop advanced from the altar to the front of the platform occupied by the choir, and stated with regret that the sermon promised by the Right Rev. Bishop Grace, of St. Paul, Minnesota, would not be delivered, owing to the unexpected illness of that revered Prelate. His Grace added that, instead of the sermon in question, he would himself address those present, first in English, and subsequently in Spanish. The Archbishop then delivered the following discourse:

THE ARCHBISHOP'S ADDRESS.

DEARLY BELOVED: This is indeed a day of joy and exultation, both to the citizens of San Francisco, and, in a certain sense, to those of the whole State of California, especially to the children of Christian light, for to-day we celebrate the Centennial of the Foundation of this Mission, and of this vast metropolis of the Pacific Coast. If our illustrious nation has justly been celebrating with rejoicing the Centennial of its existence, and the other nations of the world have been admiring the gigantic steps with which our Republic has advanced in a hundred years towards every kind of progress, with equal right and joy we are solemnizing to-day the hundredth anniversary of the existence of San Francisco as a civil and religious community, because we are especially interested in the establishment and prosperous duration of its double edifice, the foundations of which were laid in this place by our forefathers a hundred years ago.

A Centennial may be likened to a prominent, elevated spot, on which the traveller loves to rest, not only to cast a glance at the distance gained, but also to view the balance of his journey, and pursue it with fresh vigor. Thus, our Centennial affords us the pleasure of admiring the noble deeds of our ancestors, and the opportunity of encouraging ourselves to follow the course of a true civilization, and of our real and permanent interests. Others may perhaps speak of the Presidio of San Francisco developing itself in these last years into a great capital ; they may assign to it in the near future a prominent place among the cities distinguished not less for their wealth and magnificent edifices, than for their artistic and literary talent. I will endeavor to limit my few words to religious recollections, inspired not only by the present festival and hallowed spot, but also by particular persons that have come to take part in the celebration ; for we have in our midst the children of St. Ignatius, St. Francis and St. Dominic, the first Christian pioneers of both Californias, and we now occupy the same place occupied a century ago by other ministers and other people, guided by the same end, and undertaking the same work which we now have on hand—the true happiness of man through the code of the Gospel. The spiritual soldiers of Loyola had already amazed the kings of Castile and Aragon, when, few in number and with no other resources than their breviary and their apostolic charity, they conquered what the invincible Cortez and the Spanish armadas had not been able to subdue. By their charity and patience they had gained the hearts of the wild tribes of Lower California, and with arduous and apostolic labors they had established sixteen Missions in that peninsula. Sad human vicissitudes had already determined that the sons of St. Francis, and, soon after, those of St. Dominic, should succeed to the charge of these Missions; when a magnanimous heart, a great priest, a zealous apostle, desirous of the good of souls and of enriching them with the real treasures of Christian faith, the Very Rev. Father Junípero Serra, President of the Franciscan Missionaries, willingly offered to come with his fellow-laborers to found establishments of religion and Christian beneficence in this, our California. This country had never before been inhabited by civilized man; no one could vouch for his safety in it; no one had known of its fertility and immense mineral treasures. But it was known to them that in it there were souls created by the Almighty, redeemed by His divine Son, who, buried in the darkness of Paganism, had never seen the rays of the Christian light; and this was enough to induce them to undertake the great sacrifice of exiling themselves to these unexplored shores, ignorant whether it would cost them their lives, but certain that it would subject them to numberless privations and arduous labors. It is easy for us now to come and live in this land, already well known for the benignity of its climate, the fertility of its soil, its precious treasures, its magnificent edifices inhabited by persons of cultivated manners; but who can sufficiently appreciate the greatness of the sacrifice of those Franciscan Missionaries, who, guided by the spirit of Padre Junípero, or rather by that of apostolic charity, came first to live in this unknown country, among a barbarous people, who might, perhaps, repay their heroic sacrifices with ingratitude or even a fatal arrow! Yet they knew that the Son of God had not promised his Apostles any other reward in this world than that of being allowed to drink of the chalice of His passion for the benefit of man. Animated with such apostolic sentiments, those religious men came to our California, and having established the Mission of San Diego in 1769, and that of Monterey in 1770, they turned their attention to the foundation of the Mission of San Francisco.

And here I may mention the curious fact that the beautiful Bay of San Francisco was singularly discovered by land, under the auspicious exploits of the missionaries; for it had ever remained veiled to all European eyes, notwithstanding the various vessels which had periodically passed in front of the Golden Gate. Some had inclined to the opinion that Sir Francis Drake had entered our port toward the close of the sixteenth century; but it is generally held as correct, what Humboldt and De Mofras assert, that the port visited by Drake was that of Bodega, or the one bearing his name around La Punta de la Reyes. The first Europeans that ever saw our magnificent bay were those who composed the missionary expedition which came overland from San Diego, about the middle of July, 1769, to examine the already known port of Monterey; during which it happened that after the exploring party had passed the place now known as La Soledad, instead of turning west to their left, in the direction of Monterey, they continued their journey northwest, until they found themselves in full view of the Bay of San Francisco.

But the Mission of San Francisco was not founded until the 8th day of October, 1776. Three weeks before—namely, the 17th of the preceding September—the Presidio of this place had been founded with the usual formalities; and, according to the wishes and instructions of the Viceroy of Mexico, the Missionary Fathers, accompanied by the civil authorities of the Presidio, performed the memorable work of the foundation of the Mission with all possible solemnity and formality; the account of which is given us by the faithful historian and eye-witness of the ceremony, the Rev. Father Palou, in the following words:

"Being left alone with the three young men, the work of cutting timber was commenced in order to begin the construction of the chapel and houses in which to live. On the arrival of the vessel we already had sufficient timber, and with the help of some sailors furnished by Captain Quirós, in a short time a house was built thirty feet long and fifteen wide, all of plastered wood, with its roof of tule, and, adjoining it, of the same materials, a church was built fifty-two feet long, with a room for the sacristy behind the altar; and it was adorned in the best way possible with various kinds of drapery, and with the banners and pennants of the vessel. On the 8th of said month, the Lieutenant having arrived the evening before, the foundation took place, at which assisted the gentlemen of the vessel, with all the crew (except those necessary to guard the vessel), as well as the commander of the Presidio, with all the soldiers and people, retaining in the fort only the most necessary. I sang the Mass, with ministers, which, being ended, a procession was formed, in which was borne an image of our Seraphic Father, St. Francis, the patron of the Port, of the Presidio and of the Mission. The solemnity was celebrated with repeated salutes of fire-arms, and the swivel-guns which had been brought over from the vessel for the purpose, as also by the firing of rockets."

Thus, a hundred years ago, on this spot, with solemn Mass and festive procession, with holy blessings and the *Te Deum*, the standard of the Cross was elevated, the law of the Gospel was pro-claimed, the work of conversion and civilization of the gentiles was solemnly inaugurated.

I should now beg leave to examine the means adopted by our forefathers to accomplish the noble object which they proposed to themselves, or rather the general system and special laws en-acted and executed by our Christian ancestors, for the Christian civilization—the temporal and eternal welfare of the Indians. In order to have an affair of such magnitude duly attended to, the Spanish crown had constantly attached to its court

A ROYAL COUNCIL,

Composed of men distinguished for their wisdom, prudence and rectitude. This Council was especially devoted to the welfare of the Indians; and to that end it was guided by a special provision in the last will and testament of Queen Isabella "the Catholic," which deserves to be written in letters of gold. In that order she declares that, in taking possession of the islands and lands of the ocean, her principal intention was " to endeavor to induce and bring the inhabitants thereof and to convert them to our Holy Catholic faith, and to send to said islands and continent prelates and *religious* clergymen, and other persons learned and fearing God, in order to instruct the inhabitants thereof in the Catholic faith, and to teach them good morals, and to pay all the attention to that. I beseech my lord, the King, most affection-ately, and I charge and command the Princess, my daughter, and the Prince, her husband, that they perform and fulfill that, and that this be their principal aim, and bestow much care to it; and that they never consent to tolerate that the Indians and inhabitants of those islands and continent, discovered or to be discovered, receive any injury in their persons or property, but that they enjoin that they may be well and justly treated, and that they remedy any wrong which they may have received." It is not possible that Blackstone, the celebrated English jurist, in laying down the laws of equity which should guide princes in their conquests of American countries and peoples, may have studied them in the Testament of Isabella; yet, no doubt, he was guided by the principles of right embodied in the ancient digests of Christian jurisprudence, when he established the maxim, that "European princes, or their subjects, by coming to occupy the soil of the Gentile natives, did not thereby become the owners of their lands, and that if the object of bringing them to Christian civilization gave them some right, this was not that of seizing their lands, but that of buying them first with preference to others."

This is the principle which prevails throughout the Code of the *Recopilacion de Leges de Indias.* For, in the first place, it is obvious that in those laws the rights of the Indians to their lands are clearly respected according to the prescriptions of the Code, which direct that the assignment of lands to Spaniards be made without injury to the Indians, and that such as may have been granted to their injury or inconvenience be restored to them to whom they rightfully belong. The same is established by the following law:

"We ordain that the sale, benefice and composition of lands be made in a manner that to the Indians be left in abundance all such as may belong to them, both as their individual and their community lands."

And in order that the Indians might be better protected in their rights to lands, and might not easily lose them by selling them without close reflection, it was prescribed that they could not sell their lands except before a magistrate; and that even after the sale they might rescind the contract within thirty days and retain their lands, if they wished; and that if the lands of the Indians had been occupied by others, even for the space of nine years, they should be restored to them. It is also decreed that the settlers be not allowed to establish themselves near the lands of the Indians, or to have near them cattle which may injure their crops; and should this injury accidentally occur, the Indians must be fully compensated, besides their perfect liberty to kill any cattle doing **them any** injury. And although it was deemed necessary for the **civilization** and welfare of the Indians to **induce** them **to** form **towns** while cultivating **their** lands, having **in them their church and instruction, and their own** magistrates, **the statutes provide that besides their houses and** gardens **in the towns, they should retain their right to** other lands **belonging to them; and that when they would** change domicile, **and would** freely **move to** other places of their own **will, the** authorities should not prevent them, but should allow them to live and remain in them, it being at **the** same time forbidden to force them **to move from one place to another.** In their towns they **were to be induced to practice some trades, business or employment suitable to them, particularly agriculture; and in order that they should not be** molested, **it was rigorously forbidden to the Spaniards to dwell in** their towns; and in **a** special **manner it was also** forbidden to sell or give them wine, arms, or anything **which** might injure them **or** bring them to trouble.

It is also **worth considering what such a Code enacts in regard** to their **wars.** Instead **of** keeping them in subjection **with rigor, or** punishing **them with** severity in their rebellious **commotion, we** find **that the Emperor** Charles **V. enjoins on all viceroys,** judges and **governors, that if any Indians would rise in rebellion,** they **ought to** strive **to** reduce **them and to** attract them to the royal **service** with mildness and peace, without war, theft or deaths; and that they **must** observe **the laws** given by him for **the good government of the Indians,** and good treatment of the natives, **granting them some liberties if** necessary, **and** forgiving them the crimes **of rebellion committed by** them, **even** if **they** were against His Imperial Majesty and **royal service.** And should they be the aggressors, and being **armed, should** they **commence to** make war on the peaceable settlers **and** their towns, even then, **the** necessary intimations should be made to **them** once, twice and three times, and more, if necessary, **until they** be brought to the desired peace.

The same Code contains many enactments regarding **the** good treatment of the Indians; for instance, **it** recommends to all the

authorities, and even to the viceroys, the care of providing for
them, and of issuing the necessary orders that they be protected,
favored, and overlooked in their failings, in order that they may
live unmolested and undisturbed, seeing to the severe punishment of the transgressors molesting them. It especially charges
the Attorneys-General to watch particularly over the observance
of the laws enacted for their instruction, protection, good treatment and prosperity, while it is provided that they may have in
their towns their own Mayor and Supervisors, elected by themselves, and that an official, high in dignity, should visit, among
others, the towns of the Indians at least every three years, and
see that they be not ill-treated in anything. Finally, for their
greater protection, it was decreed by the King that there be
protectors and defenders of the Indians; that these be prudent
and competent men, and that they perform their duties with the
Christian spirit, disinterestedness and prompt attention with
which they are obliged to assist and defend them.

Consequently, there can be no doubt that this precious Code
of the *Recopilacion* reflects throughout the true spirit of
Christian charity to which the Indians are entitled, as the
aboriginal owners of their lands, and as men created by the same
God who made us, ransomed by the same Redeemer that saved
us, and destined, like all others, to the same heaven. But, it
may be said that, notwithstanding the spirit of Christian civilization pervading the Code, its laws were frequently disregarded,
and the Indians had much to suffer from the Spanish settlers.
Be that as it may, there can be no doubt that most, if not all, of
the Spanish monarchs were sincerely anxious, and took proper
measures to see the natives of America protected and attracted
to Christian civilization. This is particularly true of Queen
Isabella, in whom, Prescott observes, the Indians found an
efficient friend and protector. Then, the immense distance
intervening betweeen the colonies and the Mother Country must
have naturally prevented the vigorous enforcing and perfect
observance of the laws; yet the same author tells us that Car-
dinal Ximenes' eye penetrated to the farthest limits of the monarchy. He sent a commission to Hispañola to inquire into and

ameliorate the condition of the natives. And, when the natives were oppressed, there were not wanting some Las Casas, who bravely espoused

THE CAUSE OF THE OPPRESSED,

Frequently crossed the Atlantic to acquaint the Crown with the real evils, made the halls of kings ring with their loud and eloquent appeals in behalf of the Indians, secured just measures, and obtained visitors and protectors to examine and redress the wrongs. It was, no doubt, due to such measures and vigilance that the Indians were not only preserved, but frequently advanced to a comparatively good state of civilization. One of the latest writers on Our Continent, Mr. Charles Mackay, observes that "in Mexico and South America they still thrive." "They," says Sothern, "enjoyed for many generations a greater exemption from physical and moral evil than any other inhabitants of the globe." "We were exceedingly struck," says Stephens, on the descendants of the Caribs, "with the great progress made in civilization by these descendants of cannibals, the fiercest of all Indian tribes." Throughout South America, millions of the natives have been preserved and considerably advanced to the knowledge and manners of Christian civilization, under the influence of good laws and Christian instructors, while nine-tenths of the people of Mexico have been similarly benefited.

But to return to our California and our Missions. It is pleasing to find in their fresh records that, within a very short time, many missionary establishments were erected, and thrived, each being directed by two Franciscan Fathers, under whom numerous tribes of Indians were daily instructed in the lessons of Christianity; some easy trades were practised, large tracts of land were tilled, luxurious orchards and vineyards gladdened the country; and the whole coast, from Sonoma to San Diego, was alive with countless herds of cattle of every description. There were then no hotels in the country; each Mission was situated some forty miles from the nearest one, and afforded hospitable entertainment to travellers, who could go with perfect safety from one end of the country to the other. The twenty-one Missions were so many patriarchal settlements or communities of Indians, each ranging from 1,500 to 2,500, each individual working for all, all working for each, and all enjoying peace and plenty. In 1834, the crops of the twenty-one Missions came up to 122,500 bushels of grain, while the head of horned cattle belonging to the same numbered 424,000, all for the exclusive benefit of the inmates of those Missions, which numbered at that date 30,600 souls, truly blessed with plenty, but still more blessed on account of their acquired habits of industry, their daily Christian instruction and the practical lessons of morality constantly inculcated to them. Well may California be proud of her heroic, disinterested Christian pioneers, who in a short time transformed numberless barbarous tribes into comparatively well-civilized Christian communities; and well may we echo to-day with sweet strains of joyous melody the solemn *Te Deum* intoned here for the first time one hundred years ago.

In conclusion, let me pray that the Mission of the Franciscans—the establishing of Christianity in this country—may ever prove successful, and that our prosperous city may ever be favored with God's choicest benedictions, which will be the case if its citizens will be guided by the Christian counsels inaugurated here a century ago. Christian principles will insure peace and happiness, and good moral Christian lives will keep the state of society in a sound and prosperous condition. The code of the Gospel is the code of the sovereign legislator, who has an absolute right to enforce it, who demands our humble submission to it, and who has declared that on our compliance with its provisions depends our happiness, temporal and eternal. It is obvious that we shall not witness the next Centennial here; but I hope and pray that we all may see it from on high, celebrated here again with Christian spirit and becoming solemnity.

After divine service a procession was formed of the various civic and military organizations and citizens anxious to participate in the celebration. The "advance," consisting of a platoon of mounted police and six trumpeters of the United States Army, also mounted, was led by James R. Kelly, Grand Marshal, with regalia of white and yellow scarf, gold stars and fringe, American shield, red, white and blue rosettes, hat trimmed with gold lace cord and acorns, gold stars, white and black plume. The Chief Aids of the Grand Marshal were Hon. John Hamill and Hon. John M. Burnett, with regalia of red scarf, gold stars and white fringe, red, white and blue rosettes, red and white plume; and the Chief of Staff, P. J. Sullivan, with regalia of red and white scarf, trimmed with gold stars and fringe, and red plume. The Aids, with regalia of white scarfs, trimmed with blue and silver, red, white and blue rosettes and white plumes, were: A. H. Loughborough, J. T. Ryan, Daniel Sheerin, John H. Blaney, Hon. Michael Hawkins, Dr. L. Paw- licki, F. X. Kast, John Sullivan, J. J. O'Brien, John Kelly, Jr., J. P. Landers, Jeremiah F. Sullivan, W. T. Ryan, Stephen McGillan, John Reynolds, Nicholas Sweeney, Louis S. Kast, Denis Mahoney, James Regan, Wm. Sullivan, P. J. Sullivan, M. C. Hassett, William Bamber, John B. Lewis, John Shea, L. Ryan, Carroll Cook, H. Gadsby, John Fitzgerald, Thomas Kearney, Dr. F. A. A. Belinge, M. J. Kast, Mich'l Kane, M. D. Connolly, P. J. Tobin, Mathew Sullivan, Ed- ward Patten, Bernard Patten, Patrick Gallagher, J. W. McCormick, Frank Rielly, Alfred R. Kelly, C. Curtin, Thomas Pendergast, W. D. O'Sullivan, Peter Mulloy, P. H. McInerny, Charles B. Mahon, Henry Wempe, B. Dryer, James Badger, Eugene Hughes, Nicholas Wynne, Isidro Velazco, John Hill,

P. J. Thomas, M. Byrne, Edward J. Buckley,
Vincent Buckley, J. F. Sullivan, W. T. Sullivan, W.
A. Plunkett, H. A. Owen, John F. Reilly, David Land-
ers, Chas. F. Hanlon, Patrick Cummins, Carlos
Gaxiola, J. M. Tinoco, Eusebio Molera, Juan Cebrian,
M. Noe, M. Short, Hon. Herman Ranken, Dr. Francis
O'Kane, Martin J. Aguirre, Master Geo. Horan, Rob-
ert Sullivan, Patrick Tobin, John L. Murphy, Denis
Lynch, F. C. Belden, James Hatch, John C. McDon-
nell, D. Sweeney, A. J. Griffith, T. J. Powers, Thomas
D. Reardon, J. J. Donovan, P. F. Butler, James
Brennan, M. J. Egan, Thomas J. Sheerin, J. B. Law-
ton, J. J. McDonnell, John O'Kane, Martin Quinlan,
P. G. Galpin, J. H. Dougherty, J. M. Harrald, J. J.
McKinnon, Wm. J. Boerman, Aug. Tillman, D. M.
Dunne, Thomas McGrath, John Dalton, Thomas D.
Riley, T. J. Reardon, Charles Duane, Wm. Higgins,
David L. Mahoney.

The procession moved on in the following order:

FIRST DIVISION.—Military Escort; Colonel Wason, Command-
ing. Major P. R. O'Brien and Staff; First Battalion Cavalry,
Second Brigade, N. G. C.; Lieutenant William Corcoran; Pay-
master Fitzpatrick; Surgeon, Dr. Stewart; Q. M. Second Lieut-
enant James W. Collins; Adjutant, Lieutenant J. P. Rafferty.
Jackson Dragoons, Captain Michael Greany, Commanding;
Lieutenant E. McPhillips; Lieutenant J. Kennealy; Lieutenant
P. F. McGrath.

THIRD INFANTRY REGIMENT, N. G. C.—Colonel A. Wason;
Lieutenant-Colonel M. C. Bateman; Major J. J. Conlin; Adju-
tant P. J. Tannian; Quartermaster John Grant; Paymaster John
T. McGeoghegan; Commissary J. G. McGuire; Surgeon Thomas
Green; Chaplain Rev. Thomas Larkin; Sergeant-Major Con.
Donohoe; Quartermaster Sergeant Joseph Wallace; Co. A, Mont-

gomery Guard, Captain **Charles** Quinn; Co. B, Shields Guard, Captain M. J. **Wrin**; **Co. H,** McMahon Grenadier Guard, **Captain** J. H. McMenomy; Co. **D,** Meagher Guard, Captain **D. Sullivan;** Co. **C,** Wolf Tone **Guard,** Captain **T.** Fitzpatrick; Co. **E, Emmet** Life **Guard, Captain** Robert Cleary.

SECOND DIVISION. — Marshal, Wm. **D. O'Sullivan;** Regalia, **Blue scarf, trimmed with gold stars and** fringe **and** rosette; **Aids, Robert Sullivan and Edward** J. Buckley; Regalia, same as **General Aids,** but with red plumes; Four-horse Barouches, containing Governor Irwin, President of the Day; Major-Gen. **Vernon** and staff; Brigadier-Gen. John McComb and **staff;** Representatives **of the U. S. Government; Hon. J. M. Coghlan, District Attorney; Hon. T. B. Shannon, Collector of the Port; Gen. O. H. La Grange, Sup't U. S. Mint; Gen. Coey, Postmaster; Wm. Sherman, U. S. Assistant Treasurer, R. Tobin, Jr., and** others. Orators—**Hon. John W.** Dwinelle, **General M. G.** Vallejo; Reader of **the Poem, B. P. Oliver;** Mounted Cadets of St. Mary's College, **Mounted** Cadets of Sacred Heart College, escorting Archbishop **Alemany and** Bishop **O'Connell. Ba**rouches, **containing State** Officers, Mayor **A. J. Bryant,** Mayors **of San José and other cities;** Members **of the Board of** Supervisors; **Members of the Board of Education;** Foreign Consuls; City **and** County **officials; Invited Guests;** California Pioneers; Secretary P. A. **Josephs;** Reception Committee.

THIRD DIVISION.—Mounted Buglers; Reception Committee; **Marshal,** Isidro **Velasco; Aids,** Carlos Gaxiola, J. M. Tinoco; **Escort, Spanish citizens, mounted,** and Juarez Guard, Clergy, **Societies and Congregation of the Church of** Nuestra Señora de Guadalupe.

FOURTH DIVISION.—Band; Marshal, **P. J.** McKenna; Aids, **John** Reddan, P. Donohue; Clergy, **Societies and** Congregation **of Mission Dolores.**

FIFTH DIVISION.—Band; Marshal, **Hon.** Michael Hawkins; Aids, **Vincent P. Buckley, P.** J. Tobin; Independent McMahon Guard, Captain **Bryan,** Commanding; Knights of St. Patrick; Sons of the Emerald **Isle;** Laborers' Protective and Benevolent Associations.

SIXTH DIVISION—ANCIENT ORDER OF HIBERNIANS.

Band; State Officers; Thaddeus Flanagan, S. D., Marshal; Jas. F. Meagher, S. S., Assistant-Marshal; Henry Monahan, S. T., Assistant-Marshal.

San Francisco County — J. J. Donovan, C. D.; John H. Gilmore, G. P.; Jas. Collopy, G. V. P.; John E. Donovan, G. S.; John J. Lane, G. A. S.; M. J. Crowley, G. T.; P. O'Day, P. D. Winter, B. McHugh, Jas. McMenomy, Aids.

Division No. 1.—Band; James Hogan, P.; John O'Kane, V. P.; T. W. O'Brien, R. S.; Jeremiah O'Brien, F. S.; William McLaughlin, T.; John J. Lane, P. McDermot, T. Ford, J. McCloskey, Aids.

Division No. 2,—Band; Wm. Simpson, P.; B. McDermott, V. P.; M. C. Gorham, R. S.; John Killgariff, F. S.; C. O'Connor, T.; Jas. Cahill, Daniel Sheerin, M. Reilly, Jas. Collins, Aids.

Division No. 3.—John Gallagher, P,; Thos. M. Connolly, V. P.; M. O'Meara, R. S.; Thos. Flood, F. S.; Chas. Farrelly, T.; F. McCarthy, C. Farrelly, J. Linehan, Aids.

Division No. 4.—Thos. Kendrick, P.; T. D. Sullivan, V. P.; James Guilfoyle, R. S.; P. McGuigan, F. S.; Wm. Deeny, T.; Michael Murray, Charles Field, Michael Connell, John Clifford, Aids. *

Division No. 5.—John Gurry, P.; P. J. Carr, V. P.; L. Flanagan, R. S.; James McDermott, F. S.; John Curran, T.; P. J. Carr, M. Linehan, M. Maher, Aids.

Division No. 6.—Michael Hogan, P.; D. Monahan, V. P.; John Judge, R. S.; Patrick Rush. F. S.; Thomas Donnelly, T.; Thomas Donnelly, M. McFeeley, M. McCall, Aids.

Division No. 7.—E. W. McCarthy, P.; James W. Gillen, V. P.; Alphonse Murphy, R. S.; James H. Bellew, F. S.; M. G. Sears, T.; J. Barry, P. Kearney, Aids.

Division No. 8.—John Kenny, P.; D. J. Delay, V. P.; Thomas Flynn, R. S.; W. M. Gillespie, F. S.; P. Canavan, T.; C. T. Butler and C. B. McHugh, Aids.

Division No. 9.—J. M. Dwyer, P.; John H. Ryan, V. P.; Joseph W. Maher, R. S.; John F. Meagher, F. S.; Geo. O'Conner, T.; Thos. Mulvey and Robert Davis, Aids.

Solano County.—John Noonan, **C. D.**

Division **No. 1,** Vallejo—Michael **O'Keefe,** P.; John Hollo-
way, V. P.; **Jas. A.** Kane, **R. S.; Edward** Champion, F. S.; John
E. Kennedy, **T.**

Santa Clara County.—John Paine, **C. D.**

Division No. 1, San José—Denis Corkery, **P.; Michael** Nihill,
V. P.; Thomas Curran, R. S.; J. S. Curran, F. S.; John
McQuaid, T.

Division **No. 2,** Santa Clara—John Cotter, **P.**; Patrick **Gra-**
ham, V. P.; Peter Carroll, R. S.; Andrew **Dempsey,** F. **S.; L. C.**
Flynn, T.

Division **No. 3, Gilroy—Jas. Herbert, P.; Jno. Shanahan, R.
S.; Wm.** Fitzgerald, **F. S.;** Michael **Casey, T.**

Marin County.—Peter **Brunty, C. D.; Michael** Coughran, **G.
P.;** Edward Brady, **G. and P.; John Leahy, G. S.; C.** McDonald,
G. A. S.; P. Mulraney, **T.**

Division **No. 1, San** Rafael—John **Murray,** P.; Bernard
Reilly, **V. P.; Michael Dunleavy,** R. S.; **Charles** Moran, F. **S.;**
Thomas **Gordon, T.**

Division No. 2, Tomales—John Carroll, P.; John **McGinty,**
V. **P.; J. D. Connolly,** R. **S.; Robt. Mulreany, F. S.;** James
Fields, **T.**

Alameda County.—Patrick **Mullan, C. D.; S.** C. Cronin, G.
P.; Patrick Smith, G. V. P.; **John Coyle, G. S.;** Patrick Cole-
man, G. A. S.; Patrick Donohue, G. T.

Division No. 1, Oakland.—Patrick **Murphy,** P.; John Brazil,
V. P.; Jas. Leonard, R. S.; John Bryan, F. S.; Eugene Lynch, **T.**

Division No. 2, **Oakland.—James Keys, P.;** Patrick McQuade,
V. P.; John Fitzsimmons, **R. S.; C.** Mulvey, **F. S.;** Patrick
Kearney, T.

Division **No. 3,** Livermore—John Regan, **P.;** John Connolly,
R. S.; Patrick **Croke, F. S.;** Patrick Callahan, **T.**

SEVENTH DIVISION.—Band; Marshal, **J. J.** O'Brien; Aids, Hon.
Herman Ranken, Hon. **P.** G. Galpin; St. Joseph's Benevolent
Society of St. Mary's Cathedral; St. Joseph's Society of Oak-

4

land; Band; St. Mary's T. A. B. & L. Society; St. Mary's T. A.
B. Society; St. Aloysius Society; Clergy and Congregation of
St. Mary's Cathedral.

EIGHTH DIVISION.—Band; Marshal, W. A. Plunkett; Aids, S.
Ryan, August Tillman; St. Joseph's Benevolent Society of St.
Francis' Church; Clergy and Congregation of St. Francis'
Church.

NINTH DIVISION.—Band; Marshal, Col. Peter Donahue; Aids,
John O'Kane, William Hawkins, F. Wally; St. Patrick's Cadets,
Capt. Hanlon, commanding; Boys of St. Patrick's Sunday
School, D. E. Kelly, commanding; St. Patrick's Temperance
and Benevolent Society; Clergy and Congregation of St. Patrick's
Parish.

TENTH DIVISION.—Band; Marshal, B. Dryer; Aids, H. Wempe,
L. S. Kast; St. Peter's Benevolent Society; St. Paul's Benevolent
Society; Clergy and Congregation of St. Boniface Church.

ELEVENTH DIVISION.—Marshal, J. F. Sullivan; Aids, James
Hatch, Edward Patten; Sodality of the B. V. M.; Student
Sodality B. V. M.; Clergy and Congregation of St. Ignatius'
Church; Visiting Delegations from Country Parishes—Vallejo,
Benicia, Stockton, San José, Santa Clara, etc.

TWELFTH DIVISION.—Band; Marshal, Edward Dunphy; Aids,
Edward Durkin, P. Molloy; St. Joseph's T. A. and Benevolent
Society; St. Joseph's Library Society; Clergy and Congregation
of St. Joseph's Parish.

THIRTEENTH DIVISION.—Band; Marshal, Denis Mahoney; Aids,
J. P. Landers, J. T. Ryan; St. Bridget's T. A. and Benevolent
Society; Marshal, T. H. Gallagher; Aids, Jas. Farley, P. Hayes;
Clergy and Congregation of St. Bridget's Parish; Marshal,
Captain Ashwell; Aids, J. Reynolds, T. J. Sheerin; St. John
Baptist's Society; Clergy and Congregation of St. John's Parish.

FOURTEENTH DIVISION.—Band; Marshal J. J. Moore; Aids, A.
B. Maguire, Owen Daily, M. Quirk; St. Peter's Catholic T. A.
and Benevolent Society; Clergy and Congregation of St. Peter's
Parish.

FIFTEENTH DIVISION.—Marshal, Daniel Sheerin; Aids, Dr. L.
Pawlicki, Charles F. Hanlon; Citizens Mounted; Citizens in
Carriages.

At the command of the Grand Marshal the trum-
pets sounded the advance, and the procession moved
along Dolores to Sixteenth street, thence to Valencia, Market, and Kearny streets, and the old Plaza,
now beautified by ornamental trees and shrubbery,
and known as Portsmouth square. The countermarch
was by the right to Market, Eighth, and the Mechanics'
Pavilion on Mission and Eighth streets. At this point
the procession was reviewed by the Grand Marshal,
who, subsequently, on entering the Pavilion, intro-
duced his Excellency the Governor of California as
President of the Day. At least eleven thousand
persons were assembled in the vast hall. Every
seat on the floor and in the galleries was occupied,
besides all standing room within a radius of the
balcony. The Spanish, Mexican and South American elements were largely represented in the immense throng, which was graced by the presence of
many members of the clergy of the Province. There
were present in the orchestra, among other prominent
citizens, his Grace the Most Rev. Archbishop Alemany,
the Right Rev. Bishop O'Connell, of Marysville, his
Honor Mayor Bryant; Hon. John W. Dwinelle and
General M. G. Vallejo, the orators of the occasion,
County Judge Selden S. Wright; D. J. Oliver and
D. T. Murphy, Knights of the Order of St. Gregory;
Hon. Thomas B. Shannon, Collector of the Port of
San Francisco, W. C. Burnett, City and County
Attorney, Camillo Martin, Consul of Spain, Señor
Casanueva, Consul General of Chili, Señor Tinoco,
Consul of Costa Rica, Col. Peter Donahue, Gustave

Touchard and Señor de Fossas. Suspended from the gallery above the orchestra was the portrait of Father San Francisco Solano, belonging to the Pioneer Society. The painting in question, which represents the Missionary in the habit of a follower of St. Francis de Asis, with a crucifix in one hand and a violin in the other, has been pronounced a genuine one, having, it is stated, been executed in 1770, on the day when the Mission at Carmel was founded, by Don Cristoval Diaz, Chaplain of the ship *San Carlos*, which conveyed the explorers from Mexico to the then *terra incognita* of Upper California, and was the first vessel of the Spanish settlers to enter the Golden Gate. The music was rendered under the direction of Professor Toepke, organist and conductor of the choir of St. Mary's Cathedral. Although, in consequence of the pressure of time, the programme was not strictly adhered to, the military bands and an orchestra of twenty-five performers, aided by a well-trained choir of more than a hundred boys from the Sacred Heart and St. Mary's Colleges—institutes which owe their wide fame and prosperity to the rare ability, refined scholarship and indomitable energy of the Rev. Brother Justin, Superior of the Brothers of the Christian Schools in California—gave general satisfaction. The following selections were performed: Two marches by the band; "Columbia, the Gem of the Ocean;" a sparkling composition by Lambillotte, the choral and orchestral effects of which told grandly; and the ever-welcome "Star-Spangled Banner." The proceedings at the Pavilion were fitly opened by the

Grand Marshal, **James R. Kelly, who,** in well-chosen and graceful **terms,** congratulated **all** who had participated in the celebration, that **the day fraught** with **glorious recollections** had passed **off so auspiciously, and that upon an occasion so memorable, the Chief Magistrate of the Golden State and his Grace the Archbishop of San** Francisco were **present. His Excellency** the Governor said:

" We are assembled here to commemorate the planting of this Mission in San Francisco. One hundred years ago, where this great city now stands, was seen nothing but a bleak waste of sandhills and chaparral, without inhabitants, unless a few aborigines be taken into account. On the site where this Mission was founded has sprung up our great city, which is one of the great cities of commerce on the American continent, and may be regarded as both a focal and brilliant point of intelligence and power in the entire world. When I speak of San Francisco as a centre of commerce, as a seat of a civilized power, I repeat what has become axiomatic, and what every intelligent man now recognizes. You number to-day perhaps 250,000; it may be more than that; but the position of this great city in the economy of the world is destined to be of the greatest importance; and perhaps its position will ultimately give it a greater influence in the world than any other centre of population now in existence. The connection between the date of the planting of this civilization and the Centennial year which now assembles us for commemoration, affords a pleasant task for the orators who have been selected for this occasion; and with reference to them I hardly need observe that they will discharge their duty well and eloquently. Before taking my seat, I wish to state that Bishop Amat, of Monterey and Los Angeles, sends greeting to the people of San Francisco, and expresses his regret that his infirm health has prevented him from being with us on this occasion. He has, however, deputed the Rev. Hugh P. Gallagher to represent him."

The subjoined Poem, written by Miss Harriet M. Skidmore, was then read by B. P. Oliver:

'Tis well to ring the pealing bells,
  And sing the joyous lay,
And make this glad Centennial year
  One gleeful gala-day.
For Freedom's sun, that floods the land
  With Summer's golden glow,
Dawned brightly on the night of gloom,
  One hundred years ago.

And, dwellers in this favored land,
  Beside the Western sea,
Be yours an added thrill of joy,
  A two-fold jubilee !
For (sweet and strange coincidence!)
  The bright benignant glow
Of Faith dispelled a deeper gloom
  One hundred years ago!

All honor to our noble sires,
  The tried and true-souled band,
Whose valor loosed the Gordian knot
  That bound their native land;
Who crushed the tyrant's haughty host
  And laid his standard low,
And bade the starry banner wave,
  One hundred years ago !

All honor, too, and deathless fame,
  Unto the brown-robed band
Whose hands released from fetters dread
  Our glorious Golden Land;
Who gained a bloodless victory
  Against the demon foe,
And lifted high the Cross of Faith,
  One hundred years ago !

The sons of Francis journeyed far,
  From wave-washed Monterey,
To labor where his saintly name
  Had blessed our shining Bay.

And well those holy toilers wrought
  To bid Faith's harvests glow,
And Truth's sweet vineyards ripen fair,
  One hundred years ago !

Nor San Francisco saw alone
  That fondly toiling band—
Their Missions blessed full many a spot
  Within our favored land.
And Peace divine, at their behest,
  Here arched her sacred bow
From North to South, from East to West,
  One hundred years ago !

And not alone *one* chosen clime
  Obeyed their meek control—
In Earth's remotest realms they wrought
  To tame the savage soul.
From many a land that wondrous band
  Had chased the fiendish foe,
Long ere they won sweet conquest here,
  One hundred years ago !

How blessed the children of the wild
  Beneath their gentle sway !
Not theirs the harsh command that bids
  The trembling slave obey;
Not theirs the stern, despotic tone,
  The tyrant's cruel blow;
By love, the meek Franciscans ruled
  One hundred years ago !

Ah ! well the ransomed savage loved
  The kind paternal care,
That, with his simple joy could smile,
  And in his sorrows share;
That could the blest baptism give—
  The Bread of Life bestow—
And cheer the darksome vale of Death,
  One hundred years ago.

Within the rude adobe shrine,
  What holy calmness dwelt !
How fervent was the savage throng
  That round its altar knelt !

How lowly bowed the dusky brows
    When, through the sunset glow,
Rang out the sweet-toned Angelus,
    One hundred years ago !

Pure, Eden-like simplicity,
    Forever passed away !
For o'er the Missions came at last,
    A fierce tyrannic sway—
A sacrilegious hand could dare
    To strike with savage blow,
The band that brought Salvation's boon
    One hundred years ago !

But we, who know how rich the gift
    That holy land bestowed
Upon the land where stranger hosts
    Since made their fair abode—
Aye, we who hail the beams of Faith,
    In radiant, noonday glow,
Will fondly bless the dawn that rose
    One hundred years ago !

O Sovereign City of the West,
    Enthroned in royal state,
Where bows the Bay its shining crest,
    Within thy Golden Gate,
Thou'lt ne'er forget, though o'er thy heart
    Vast, living currents flow,
The herald-steps that trod thy soil,
    One hundred years ago!

And though the lofty steeples rise
    From many a sunlit hill,
Where, through the air, at dusk and dawn,
    The sweet bell-voices thrill,
Thou'lt fondly prize thy Mission shrine—
    For o'er its portal low,
First rose the Cross, and rang the chime,
    One hundred years ago !

Hon. John W. Dwinelle delivered, amid frequent bursts of applause, **the oration which follows:**

EXCELLENT GOVERNOR,

ILLUSTRIOUS ARCHBISHOP,

REVEREND CLERGY,

LADIES AND GENTLEMEN :

One hundred and seven years ago, in **the** year seventeen hundred and sixty-nine, the compact territory which **now** constitutes the great body of the United **States might have been thus described,** for general **purposes:**

A tract bounded by the Atlantic Ocean, the northern lakes and the Mississippi River, with the Spanish peninsula of Florida lying at the southeast. A portion of Mexico, called Upper California (Alta California), extending northward from the latitude of San **Diego along the Pacific Coast** toward the uncertain boundary **of the British Provinces above** Oregon, **and** with a contested **boundary on the east. Between the two, and** bounded **by each, abutting upon the Gulf of Mexico on the** south, including **the present State of Louisiana , and the im-** mense **tract** west **of the Mississippi, a vast wedge-shaped** territory **belonging to the King of Spain, but afterwards trans-** ferred **to France.**

CALIFORNIA ONE HUNDRED YEARS AGO.

One hundred and seven years ago, in the year 1769, California was a desert wilderness. Its coasts had been explored by Spanish navigators, who had given names to its prominent points, but throughout its vast territory, more than 800 miles in **extent** from south to north, there was **no cabin** or tent of the white man, no vestige of his presence, no physical trace **of** his existence. The bay of San Francisco, the most marked and marvellous feature in the northwestern **line of** the continent, had not been discovered. A delusive cloud generally brooded over the entrance of the Golden Gate, like **the magic** mist obscuring the entrance to the treasures of an oriental **fable.** Even Sir Francis Drake, who, in the year 1578, after having committed piratical

*4

plunder upon the Spanish galleons bearing the treasures of the
kings of Spain from Manilla to Acapulco, fled to the north, hoping
to escape the vengeance of his pursuers by finding and navigating
a northeast passage to the Atlantic Ocean, sailed ignorantly
across the vast volume of the Sacramento and San Joaquin rivers,
discharging themselves into the ocean athwart the very keel of
his caravel, and whose existence, if known to him, would have
suggested to him that he had found the overland water passage
of which he was in search..

COLONIZATION BEGUN.

Precisely one hundred and seven years ago, in the year 1769,
the colonization of California had its beginning; but it was a
religious, and not a civil or political colonization; and its origin,
aims and results are to be treated as the work of the Roman
Catholic Church. As a Protestant, with my fellow Protestants,
I come here to-day, not to sing fulsome praises to the Roman
Catholic Church, but to render her a due meed of honor. When
we speak of modern colonization, the idea generally presents
itself to us of a settled, civilized State, gradually exceeding its
geographical boundaries and absorbing what lies beyond them.
But ancient colonization did not advance by any such gradual
processes. When Rome established colonies in territory conquered from Apulia or Gaul, she sent out a procession of citizens and officers, who took possession of the new territory in the
name of the parent State, whose exact image they endeavored to
reproduce on the spot. So, when Greece sent her colonists to
Magna Græcia or to Sicily, the new institutions were presumed
to be cast in the pattern of the old, and to resemble them as
children resemble their parents, or rather as twin children
resemble each other. The customs of Spain preserved all these
formalities, and devoted the soil to the new colony with acts of
equal solemnity.

THIS COLONIZATION WAS BY RELIGIOUS MISSIONS.

The motive of the colonization of California was not civil,
but religious. Its plan was not so much to bring citizens into

California, as it was to convert the native savages of California into Christians, afterwards into citizens, with **organized civil** institutions, and then leave **them in** possession of the conquered, civilized and Christian **territory;** the Missions **converted into villages, or** Pueblos, **and the Mission churches into parochial churches.** These Missions, thus **established to civilize** the **Indians, were to be fortified against hostile** incursions by military **posts established on the coast,** called Presidios, and have a pattern **and a moral** support in villages or Pueblos, composed **of** married soldiers and white colonists from the main land of Mexico. The religious character of this colonization **is most** emphatically and accurately **described in the** following language of Hon. **Alpheus** Felch, one **of the first Judges** on the **United** States Land **Commission in California:**

THE MISSIONS INTENDED TO BE TEMPORARY.

"**The Missions were intended,** from the beginning, **to be** temporary in their character. It was contemplated that in ten years **from their** first foundation **they should cease.** It was supposed **that within** that period **of time the** Indians would be sufficiently **instructed in** Christianity **and the arts of civilized life to** assume **the position** and character of **citizens; that these Mission settlements would then become Pueblos, and that the** Mission **churches would become Parish** churches, **organized** like the other establish-**ments of an** ecclesiastical **character in** other portions of the **nation where no** missions had **ever existed. The** whole missionary establishment was widely different **from the** ordinary ecclesiastical organization of the nation. **In it the superintendence** and charge was **committed to priests who were devoted to the special** work of Missions, **and not the ordinary clergy. The monks** of **the** College of San **Fernando and Zacatecas, in whose** charge **they were, were to be succeeded by the secular clergy** of the **National Church, the Mission to give place to a Bishop, the Mission churches to become** curacies, **and the faithful in the vicinity of each parish to** become **the parish worshippers."**

JESUIT MISSIONS IN LOWER CALIFORNIA.

The Jesuits were the first to take charge of this work in Lower California, as far back as the year 1683. In the year 1767 they had colonized with Missions, and Christianized all that peninsula. But in that year the King of Spain carried into execution a secret resolution that on a certain day he would expel all the Jesuits from his dominions. This act reached the Jesuit missionaries in Lower California. At the concerted day and hour the Governor appeared at the Missions in Lower California, and summoned the missionaries to his presence, to surrender the Missions, together with their reputed treasures of gold and silver. His behest was answered by a few gray-haired old priests, bearing the marks of the toil and poverty which they shared with their Indian converts, who accompanied them, with tears and lamentations, to the ships which bore them away into banishment, like convicted criminals.

UPPER CALIFORNIA SURRENDERED TO THE FRANCISCANS.

The final result of this harsh procedure was that the Missions of Lower California were surrendered to the Dominicans, while the virgin field of Upper California was yielded to the Franciscans. This could not have been done at a more fortunate juncture. Father Junípero Serra, at that time President of the Franciscans in California, was a man of fervent piety, indomitable will, irrepressible energy, and unconquerable fortitude, all which qualities were concentrated into one purpose, *ir á la conquista*— to conquer souls to the dominion of the Church. Under his auspices the Mission of San Diego, the first settlement made by the whites in California, was effected on June 16th, 1769, and that of Carmel, at Monterey, on June 3d, 1770, together with two Presidios at the same points. But the establishment of these two Missions and Presidios of San Diego and Monterey, with the consequent support which they gave to the pious labors of the missionaries, did not satisfy these devoted men. Father Junípero Serra, the founder and first President of the Franciscan Missions of Upper California, and the real conqueror of this region, with that pious zeal for the salvation of souls which prompted him ever to go on with the conquest (*ir á la conquista!*), represented to the Marquis de la Croix, the then Viceroy of Mexico, that it was a reproach to Catholic Christianity that there was no Mission dedicated to San Francisco de Asis, the founder and patron of the Order which bore his name. There was a tradition among the old native Californians that the Viceroy replied: "If our Father San Francisco wants a Mission dedicated to him let him show us that good port up beyond Monterey, and we will build him a Mission there!" Long before this there was a report coming down from the early navigators, that on the northwestern coast, about a hundred miles north of Monterey, there existed a large bay, through which large volumes of fresh water were poured into the sea by rivers flowing from an unknown distance in the interior. But later explorers had not been able to find this entrance, and in the time of the Marquis de la Croix the Bay of San Francisco had become to be considered quite as apocryphal as Psalmanazar's island of Formosa, or the Antarctic Continent of Commodore Wilkes in our day. It was therefore with a feeling of prayerful humorousness that the Viceroy invoked the aid of Saint Francis in the discovery of this concealed harbor. Father Junípero, however, took the Viceroy at his word, and, by a land expedition sent from Monterey in 1772, happily established the existence of the Bay of San Francisco, which was afterwards explored by competent engineers, entering from the sea, and to which the name of San Francisco, the founder of his Order, became permanently affixed.

THE FRANCISCANS COME TO SAN FRANCISCO.

Father Francisco Palou, who, with Father Benito Cambon, was the monk that founded the Mission of San Francisco, thus continues the narrative, in his life of Junípero Serra:

"The bay of San Francisco having been re-discovered, the then Viceroy of New Spain—the Marquis de la Croix—thereupon, by an order dated November 12th, 1775, gave directions for the foundation of a Fort, Presidio and Mission upon the Bay of San Francisco. The colonists, with their cattle and the neccessary provisions for the journey, were to come by land from Monterey, while the rest of the equipments was sent from the same port by sea.

" The said overland expedition left the Presidio of Monterey on the appointed day, 17th of June, of said year of 1776. It was composed of the said Lieutenant commanding, Don José Moraga, one sergeant, and sixteen soldiers clad in leather armor—all married men with large families, of some followers and servants of the same, of herdsmen and drovers who drove the neat stock of the Presidio, and the pack-train with provisions and necessary equipage for the road, the rest of the freight being left for the vessel which was about to sail. And, as regards the Mission, we, the two missionaries above named, joined the party with two young men, servants for the Mission, two neophyte Indians of old California, and another of the Mission of San Carlos, for the purpose of trying whether he could serve as an interpreter; but as the idiom was found to be a different one, he served only to take care of the cows that were brought for the purpose of raising a stock of cattle. The said expedition came on towards this port."

The land expedition arrived first, and encamped at a pond called Dolores, a short distance east of the present site of the Mission. This spot was known as the Willows, in 1849 and afterwards, and was graded and filled in about ten years ago, occupying most of the tract enclosed by Seventeenth, Nineteenth, Valencia, and Howard streets. The incidents of the re-discovery of the Bay of San Francisco, and those attending the expeditions sent out for its colonization, are very interesting; but we have no time to narrate them in detail.

THE MISSION OF SAN FRANCISCO FOUNDED, OCTOBER 8TH, 1776.

As soon as the expedition arrived, the missionaries commenced their labors. The registers of baptisms, marriages and burials, which they began, bear date on the first day of August; but the Presidio was not founded until the 17th day of September, nor the Mission until the 8th day of October, 1776. Among the customs of Spain, none was more rigid than that which required public acts to be **executed with the greatest** notoriety and official formality. **Even a** distinguished **military** officer, like Coronado, must execute **a public,** official, notarial act when he **charged himself** with a commission **to explore a desert country, and discharge** himself **by an act of equal solemnity when he made his report. So, when a Town or Mission was founded by the Spaniards,** they **fixed the site and the day by the official celebration of** solemn **and authentic acts. And until** these acts **were performed,** the **historical facts** thus authenticated did not exist; the **town,** its name, its site, had not yet been determined; for intentions might be abandoned, plans changed, **the whole project** fail. **As,** among **the Greeks and** Romans, **the new colony was founded by tracing out with a furrow the proposed limits of the suburbs; by erecting the statue of its tutelar deity; by the scattering of corn, and the pouring out of oil and wine; so, with equal solemnity, but with a higher purpose and deeper religious sentiment, on the 8th day of October, 1776, the pious missionaries planted the Cross at the Mission of Dolores, chanted the first mass, and consecrated its soil to** Christianity **and civilization. As they then intended that the Mission** which **they thus founded should become the future Town, and as** they **chose that** date **for the performance of the official act which gave a birth, a name, and a practical existence to our city,** we must accept **their choice, and date the** anniversary **of our foundation from** the 8th day **of October, 1776.** On that **day,** and **by that act,** the Mission church, **the** orchards, and the **cemetery became the** property **of** the CATHOLIC CHURCH, **by a** title **which is far the oldest title to** land **in the city; it** completes its **first century to-day.**

DESCRIPTION OF A MISSION.

The following description, **given by** a contemporary, M. Duflot **de Mofras, will give a** very accurate notion **of the missionary** establishments :

"The building is a quadrilateral; the church occupies one of **its** wings; the façade is ornamented with a gallery. **The** building raised **some** feet above the soil, is two stories in height. The interior is formed by a court. Upon the gallery which **runs around it, open the dormitories of the** monks, **of the** overseers **and of travellers, small work-shops, school-rooms and** store-rooms. The hospitals are situated in the most quiet part of the Mission, where the schools also are kept. The young Indian girls dwell in the halls, called the nunnery, and they themselves are called nuns. Placed under the care of Indian matrons, who are worthy of confidence, they learn to make cloths of wool, cotton and flax, and do not leave the nunnery until they are married. The Indian children mingle in the schools with those of the white colonists. A certain number, chosen among the pupils who display the most intelligence, learn music, chanting, the violin, the flute, the horn, the violoncello, and other instruments. Those who distinguish themselves in the carpenter's shop, at the forge, or in agricultural labors, are appointed overseers, and charged with the direction of a squad of workmen. The administrative body of each Mission consists of two monks, of whom the elder has charge of the interior and of the religious instruction, and the younger of the agricultural works. In order to maintain morals and good order in the Mission, they employ only so many whites as are absolutely necessary, for they well know that their influence is pernicious, and that an association with them developes among the Indians those habits of gambling and drunkenness to which they are unfortunately too much inclined. The regulations of each Mission are the same. The Indians are divided into squads of laborers. At sunrise the bell sounds the Angelus, and every one sets out for the church. After mass they breakfast, and then go to work. At 11 they dine, and this period of repose extends to 2 o'clock, when they return to labor until the evening Angelus, one hour before sunset. After prayers and the rosary, the Indians have supper, and then amuse themselves with dancing and other sports. Their diet consists of fresh beef and mutton, as much as they choose; of wheat and corn cakes, fruits, and of boiled porridges called *atole* and *pinole*. They also have peas and beans—in all, the twelfth part of a bushel a week. For dress, they have a linen shirt, pantaloons and a woolen blanket; but the overseers and best workmen have habits of cloth like the Spaniards. The women receive every year two chemises, a gown and a blanket. When the hides, tallow, grain, wine, oil and other products, are sold at good prices to ships from abroad, the monks distribute handkerchiefs, wearing apparel, tobacco, chaplets and glass trinkets among the Indians, and devote the surplus to the embellishment of the churches, the purchase of musical instruments, pictures and sacerdotal ornaments. Still, they are careful to keep a part of their harvest in the granaries to provide for years of scarcity."

SUCCESS OF THE MISSIONS.

The immediate results of the Mission scheme of Christianization and colonization were such as to justify the plans of the wise statesmen who devised it, and to gladden the hearts of the pious men who devoted their lives to its execution. At the end of

sixty-five **years, (in 1834), the missionaries of Upper** California
found themselves **in possession of** twenty-one prosperous Missions, planted **upon a line of about seven** hundred miles, run
ning from San **Diego north to the latitude of Sonoma.   More**
than **thirty thousand Indian converts were lodged in the Mission
buildings, receiving religious culture, assisting at divine worship,
and cheerfully performing their easy tasks.   Over seven hundred
thousand cattle, of various species, pastured upon the plains, as
well as sixty** thousand horses.   One hundred **and twenty** thous-
and bushels **of** wheat were raised annually, **which, with maize,**
beans, peas, and the like, made up **an annual crop of one hun-**
dred and eighty thousand **bushels; while, according to the climate, the different Missions rivalled each other in the production
of wine, brandy, soap, leather, hides, wool, oil, cotton, hemp,
linen, tobacco, salt and soda.   Of two hundred thousand horned
cattle annually slaughtered, the Missions** furnished about one-
half, whose hides, hoofs, horns and tallow were sold at a net
result of about ten dollars each, making **a million dollars from
that source alone.   While the other articles,** of which **no definite**
statistics can be **obtained,** doubtless reached an equal **value, mak-**
ing a **total production by the** Missions themselves **of two million**
dollars.   Gardens, vineyards and orchards **surrounded all the**
Missions, except the **three** northernmost—Dolores, San Rafael,
and San Francisco **Solano—the** climate **of** the first being too
inhospitable for that purpose, **and the two latter, born** near the
advent of the Mexican revolution, **being stifled** in their infancy.
The other Missions, **according to their latitude, were** ornamented
and enriched with plantations of palm trees, bananas, oranges,
olives **and figs;** with orchards **of European** fruits; and with vast
and fertile vineyards, whose **products were** equally valuable for
sale and exchange, and **for the diet** and comfort of the inhabitants
of the Missions.   Aside from these valuable properties, and
from the Mission buildings, the live stock of the Missions,
valued **at their** current rates, **amounted** to three million
dollars of **the most active** capital, bringing enormous annual re-
turns upon its aggregate **value, and,** owing to the great fertility
of animals in California, more than repairing its annual waste by

slaughter. Such was the great religious success of the Catholic Missions in Upper California; such their material prosperity in the year 1834, even after many depredations had been committed upon them. These Missions were not only prosperous, but they were self-sustaining. It is true that there was a fund in Mexico of the aggregate capital of two million dollars, called

THE PIOUS FUND OF CALIFORNIA,

Which, during a century, had been gradually built up by donations from the children of the Catholic Church, and whose income was to be devoted to sustain the Catholic Missions in California. But the Missions never received any reliable assistance from that source; the proceeds of the fund were systematically embezzled; and finally, in 1842, General Santa Anna, Provisional President of Mexico, by one bold, sweeping act of robbery, confiscated the whole fund.

THE MISSIONS DOOMED TO EXTINCTION.

I have already shown that the theory of the scheme upon which the Missions were constructed was, that in the course of ten years from their establishment, the Indian converts would be so far Christianized and instructed that they could assume the condition of citizens, the Missions be converted into Pueblos or villages, and the Mission churches into Parish churches. The period thus limited had now expired; but other causes existed to provoke the Executive Act by which the Missions were to be extinguished. The prosperity of the Missions had excited the cupidity and rancor of private greed. The products of the Mission were crude, requiring but little alteration by any process of manufacture or manipulation — such as hides, tallow, horns, peltries, wool, wine, brandy, oil, olives, soap, cotton and hemp— and it was easy to exchange them, twice a year, with the skippers who visited the coast in their trading voyages, receiving in return, in honest barter, the articles most needed by the Missions, and the balance in hard silver dollars, (pesos duros). But this did not suit the views of a class of private traders who had established themselves at the ports of San Diego, Santa Barbara,

Monterey and San Francisco, and at some other points in the interior, who insisted that this exchange between the Missions and the sea merchants should pass through their hands, and pay them a profit, and who demanded, as a right for a forcibly inter-jected middleman, the same perquisities which the modern Gran-ger resists as an unnecessary tax. This new class of adventurers, characterized by the exuberance of their noses, their addiction to the social game called monté, and the utter fearlessness with which they encountered the monster aguardiente, were both constant and persistent in their denunciations of the monks who had charge of the Missions. They were accused of being avari-cious—these poor monks who had taken the vow of perpetual poverty. They were said to be indolent; they who roused them-selves at the morning *Angelus*—Summer and Winter--to perform the services of the church; and, after that, the arduous labors of the day; to whom the evening *Angelus* was only a signal that their evening task was only begun and not ended.

THE RUIN OF THE MISSIONS ACCOMPLISHED.

But the extinction of the Missions was decreed—first, by Act of Cortez of Spain in 1813; afterward by decrees of the Mexican Congress of 1828 and 1833. And so the whole system went down, and existed only in history. And then it appeared that the whole theory on which it had been built was a false one; that the American Indian could not be converted into an independent citizen. Yet the benevolent and pious plan was not utterly barren of results. It was something, surely, that over 30,000 wild, barbarous and naked Indians had been brought in from their sav-age haunts; persuaded to wear clothes; accustomed to a regular life; living in Christian matrimony; inured to such light labor as they could endure; taught a civilized language; instructed in music; accustomed to the service of the church; partaking of its sacraments, and indoctrinated in the Christian religion. And this system had become self-sustaining, under the mildest and gentlest of tutelage; for the Franciscan Friars, who superintended these establishments, most of whom were from Spain, and many of them highly cultivated men, statesmen, diplomatists, soldiers,

engineers, artists, lawyers, merchants, and physicians, before
they became Franciscans, always treated the neophyte Indians
with the most paternal kindness, and did not scorn to labor with
them in the field, the brick-yard, the forge, the tannery,
and the mill. When we view the vast constructions of the Mission buildings, including the churches, the refectories, the dormitories, the workshops, the granaries, and the rancherías, sometimes constructed with huge timbers brought many miles on the
shoulders of the Indians, and look at the massive constructions
at Santa Barbara, and the beautiful carvings and ribbed stone
arches of the church of the Carmelo, we cannot deny that the
Franciscan missionary monks had the wisdom, sagacity, learning, skill, self-sacrifice, and patience to bring their neophyte
pupils far forward on the road from barbarism to civilization, and
that these Indians were not destitute of taste and capacity.
It is enough that the Franciscan monks succeeded in all that
they undertook to accomplish. It matters not that the Spanish theory of the available capacity of the Americo-Indian races
for final self-government and independent citizenship was a false
one. After having shown that these people could be Christianized
and civilized by the attraction of kindness and the imposition of
systematic, regular and easy tasks, while in a state of pupilage,
the destruction of the Missions of California seems to have
demonstrated the converse proposition that these are the only
conditions of the proximate Christianization of these races.
Such were the opinions which the Catholic priesthood, both
regular and secular, had come to entertain, from the long
experience of the missionaries in the two Californias—opinions
which were shared by many of the most enlightened statesmen
of Mexico. The political decrees which destroyed the Missions
of California were ordained in the face of the remonstrances of
the Roman Catholic Church.

SURVIVAL OF THE MISSIONS AS PAROCHIAL CHURCHES.

But although the Missions, as such, were destroyed; although
the Mission system thus disappeared, and the body of the neophytes was annihilated in one general cataclysm of drunkenness,

mendicity and disease, still some results remained, which were worth all that they cost. Taking the number of 30,000 Indians who resided in the Missions at the height of their prosperity, and estimating the average life of the Indian as a short one, as it undoubtedly was, I calculate that during the sixty-five years of the prosperity of the Missions, no less than 80,000 Christianized Indians were buried in the *Campos Santos*—the consecrated cemeteries. I estimate that during the last one hundred years no less than 20,000 whites, natives and foreign, were buried, as baptized Catholics, in the same holy soil. I know that during all this period the Mission churches filled the office of secular churches to the native and foreign white residents, and that when Protestants came into California, as emigrants, from England, Scotland, Germany and the United States, they almost always were baptized into the Catholic Church. And that when the Mission system reached its catastrophe, and the United States afterwards succeeded to the political dominion of Spain and Mexico, something more remained, which had not died, and which can never die. It was a series of Catholic churches, extending from San Diego to Sonoma, with the altars, the vestments and the paraphernalia of worship. It was the solemn registers of baptisms, marriages and burials, extending backward for a hundred years, and invoking the mysterious solemnity of religion upon those acts upon which repose domestic felicity, the security of property, and the hope of happiness beyond the grave. This was the possession which the secular church received in California—a possession which came to her by inheritance as the successor of those Missions over whose destruction she mourned. When the tide of emigration, originating from the discovery of gold in 1848, flowed in upon California, it found the Holy Roman Catholic Church occupying the soil, into which she had become rooted by the providential events of the previous one hundred years. Of the twenty-three missions established in California by the Franciscan monks, the sites of no less than nineteen, including the churches, orchards and cemeteries, have been confirmed in full ownership to the Roman Catholic Church by the authorities of the United States. These are the oldest, as they will be the most enduring, marks of civilization impressed upon the soil of California.

THE EVENTS OF A HUNDRED YEARS.

It was not without a purpose that I began this address with a description of California as it existed in 1769—one hundred and seven years ago. In that year, 1769, began those missionary settlements which resulted in the civilization of California. And about the same time commenced, on the Atlantic Coast, those political agitations which resulted in the Declaration of Independence on July 4th, 1776, and in the establishment of the American Republic. During the last one hundred years the United States of America have not only secured their own existence, but have absorbed the territory of Spanish Florida, the American dominions of France and Spain lying north of the Gulf of Mexico, and the very territory of Old Spain on the Pacific which the Franciscan Friars had colonized with their Missions.

Macaulay and Ranke, accepted historical critics, neither of them especially friendly to the Roman Catholic Church, are both of the opinion, that, after all the assaults and persecutions of the last three hundred and fifty years, she is stronger than she was in the time of Martin Luther. We will not go back three hundred and fifty years; but as we are now celebrating a centenary, we shall take the shorter period of one hundred years.

ONE HUNDRED YEARS AGO,

Among all English-speaking races, the name and faith of the Roman Catholic was proscribed. I do not know of any place where he could lawfully vote, or hold office, or exercise his faith Even in Maryland, he could not do this lawfully, but only colusively. In most places the laws were made for him by legislators whom he could have no hand in electing; who denounced him as an idolator; and who professed to hold him and his creed in abhorrence. In some places the son, by becoming an apostate, could anticipate his father's death, and enter upon his inheritance.

The Declaration of American Independence came, and with it the sentiment, incorporated into all subsequent National and State legislation, that the State has no concern with the private religious belief of the citizen. A hundred years have rolled by! The Great Democratic Empire is consolidated. It embraces in its territory the Spanish and French domain north and north-west of the Gulf of Mexico, the French Missions whose line extended from Detroit to New Orleans, and from St. Louis to the Columbia River; the Franciscan Missions from San Diego to Sonoma. But it says to all of these, to every citizen, to the Catholic Church, the State has no concern with your religious belief. Under this new régime the State has let the Church alone; not merely because it would, but because it must. The whole executive power of the 40,000,000 citizens of the United States cannot now seize a single Catholic priest, and ship him abroad as an expatriated criminal. All the legislative power of the United States cannot confiscate the stipend of the humblest Catholic missionary, nor sequestrate the revenues of the poorest Catholic Church.

THE ROMAN CATHOLIC CHURCH IN THE UNITED STATES TO-DAY.

A hundred years ago how feeble was the Catholic Church in the United States! To-day how strong she is—strongest among the strong. A hundred years ago proscribed, her name a reproach! To-day, proud in the consciousness of her strength, her children are free to ask for every thing—to receive it. They can be legislators, Governors, Senators and Judges; one of them was Chief Justice of the United States for twenty-five years. And the example of the forty million citizens of the United States has not been lost upon other peoples. Is it not true that where the English language is now spoken, the Catholic Church is practically free? That, although there may be enactments against her on the statute books, they are in effect dead, and cannot be enforced?

THE TRUE BASIS OF HER MATERIAL PROSPERITY.

Where is she stronger at this day than in the United States? Where are her foundations broader, deeper, more solid? Where are her hospitals, her convents, her colleges, her churches in a more flourishing condition ? And does this not demonstrate that her material strength lies in the law of voluntary contribution and in those free political institutions which " *let her alone ?* "

I believe that religion is necessary to the prosperity of the State. I believe that the world is more truly religious now than it was a hundred years ago. I believe that the Roman Catholics of California are more than compensated for all they have lost, in having their political destinies brought within the circle of the American Union.

THE CONTRAST OF A HUNDRED YEARS.

Behold the contrast! A hundred years ago to-day not fifty people were present when the foundation of the city of San Francisco was laid. To-day, thousands assist at the celebration of the hundredth anniversary of that event, and a million people may be said to be within reach of our voices. Then, there was absolutely no population. Now, there are upwards of 300,000. In another hundred years, of the estimated population of two hundred millions allotted to the United States, I cannot doubt that San Francisco will be the largest city on the Pacific Ocean, and that at least twenty millions will occupy territory ceded by Mexico to the American Union: nor can I doubt that on that territory the Catholic Church will maintain her comparative strength.

THE NEXT HUNDRED YEARS.

I have not, on this occasion, uttered a word in praise of the Holy Apostolic Roman Catholic Church. If I had been one of her sons, I should have given her such a tribute as full of grati- tude as of truth. But, as it is, this might seem like adulation, and she does not need to be patronized. Still less have I ventured to insult her children by apologizing for them that their faith differs from mine. But, Protestant as I am, I am not afraid to say that I rejoice in the strength and prosperity of the Holy Apostolic Roman Catholic Church ; and that when I predict that a hundred years from now she will be stronger than ever, and that her greatest strength will be in the United States, it is because my heart goes with the prediction ; and when I consider that she has been the mother of all modern civilization, and the foster-mother of all free political institutions, I devoutly invoke Almighty God that this great empire of freemen may empty into her lap the Horn of Plenty in its widest abundance.

At the conclusion of Mr. Dwinelle's oration, General Vallejo addressed the assemblage in the Spanish language, of which the following is a translation:

MR. PRESIDENT,

MOST REVEREND ARCHBISHOP,

LADIES AND GENTLEMEN:—

Honored by the cordial invitation tendered me by the Board of Directors of the present celebration, through the most Reverend Archbishop Alemany, I present myself before you for the purpose of narrating, in a few but significant words, the history of the discovery, occupation and foundation of this Mission of our holy Father, San Francisco de Asis, a name which it has borne with dignity since the time it was so called by the indefatigable missionary, Father-President Junípero Serra and companions, in respect and veneration for the founder of their Seraphic Order.

Would that I were possessed of the necessary ability to do justice to the merits of those men, to whom is due the civilization of so many thousands of souls, and of numberless others that will succeed them.

But, if my incapacity is great, my ardent desire to comply with the duty which has been imposed upon me, and which I have gladly accepted, is still greater. I only wish to ask your kind indulgence.

I shall be as brief in my discourse as a subject of such great magnitude as this is will permit. Before, however, entering into the particulars of our present subject matter, I may be permitted to give a condensed synopsis of the events by which this Port of San Francisco came into the possession of the Crown of Spain.

In the years 1542 and 1543 the navigator Cabrillo sailed up and down the coast, and passed San Francisco without having determined anything but the formation of the coast line.

5

In 1578, Sir Francis Drake, an English buccaneer, anchored and remained a month, perhaps, in the small bay on the northern extremity of the ocean or open bay of the Farallones, at the same place which was called by us the Port of Tomales. Drake gave this latter bay his name, and the surrounding country he called New Albion. There is a bare possibility of Drake's entering the present Bay of San Francisco, but the weight of evidence is against him. There is no doubt that it was in the Bay of Tomales that the vessel from China, called the *San Agustin*, was sunk in the year 1595. It is beyond contradiction that the name of San Francisco was given to the bay at that time, on account of some circumstance unknown to us ; perhaps, in honor of the Patron Saint of the day on which the vessel arrived.

It is an absurdity to suppose that there can be any connection between Sir Francis Drake and San Francisco, except in the imagination of some visionary geographer. Very little is known concerning the voyage; but the wreck of the *San Agustin* was afterwards brought by the currents into the Port of San Francisco (the Golden Gate), and as far as Yerba Buena, at Clark's Point, where I was shown fragments of the same about two hundred years after (1830), by the veteran officer Don José Antonio Sanchez.

In 1603 the Admiral Sebastian Vizcayno, having on board of his flag-ship one of the pilots of the *San Agustin*, sailed up and down the coast, stopping, without landing in the Bay of San Francisco (not the present one), which was that of Tomales, near Point Reyes. Vizcayno took very extensive and correct geographical observations; but the only copy of his chart in existence is made on such a small scale that very little information can be derived from it concerning this portion of the coast.

In subsequent years several vessels from the Philippine Islands came down the coast on their way to Acapulco ; no mention, however, is made that any of them ever touched at any point on the coast of California, although it is certain that from the voyages in question we have notes concerning its coast. By some data obtained therefrom, and particularly from the observations of Vizcayno, the first pilot of the Philippines, Don José

Gonzales Cabrera Bueno, made several sea charts which, together with a theoretical Treatise on Navigation, was published in Manilla in the year 1734. This work gives a description of the coast from Point Reyes to Point Pinos with the same degree of accuracy as can be given in the present day, with the exception of what appertains to the Golden Gate and the unknown interior of the Bay of San Francisco. In it there is described perfectly the ancient bay of the same name, near Point Reyes, as the present one was not known at that time, and not discovered until thirty-five years later.

On the 31st of October, 1769, the expedition from San Diego was the first that made explorations in California overland. In it came Portolá, Rivera y Moncada, Fages and Father Crespí. They ascended the hills now called Point San Pedro (county of San Mateo), from whence they saw the bay of the Farallones, which extends from Point San Pedro to Point Reyes ; and they also noticed Cabrera Bueno's bay of San Francisco, and the Farallones. On the 1st of November they sent a party to Point Reyes. On the 2d of the same month several hunters of the expedition ascended the high mountains more towards the east; and, although we have no correct information as to the names of those hunters, it is certain that they were the first white inhabitants who saw the large arm of the sea known at present as the Bay of San Francisco. The portion that was seen by them was that which lies between the San Bruno mountains and the estuary or creek of San Antonio (Oakland). They discovered the Bay, unless the honor is accorded to the exploring party that returned on the 3d of November, who also had discovered the branch of the sea, by which they were prevented from reaching Point Reyes, and the primitive Bay of San Francisco. On the 4th of November the whole of the expedition saw the newly discovered bay, and they tried to go around it by the south; but not being able to do so, they returned to Monterey. The next exploration had in that direction was made by Pedro Fages and Father Crespí, in the month of March, 1772, from Monterey ; and it was with the view of going around the arm of the sea reaching Point Reyes, and arriving at the Bay of San Francisco of

of the first navigators. For greater accuracy in the description
I am about to make, I ask permission to use the names by which
the places through which they passed are known at the present
day.

Fages and Father Crespí started escorted by a guard of soldiers
of the Company of Volunteers of Cataluña, and another from
that of the "Cuera," or Leather coats. They arrived at Salinas
river (to which they gave the name of Santa Delfina), crossed
it, and, passing by the site upon which is now located Salinas
City, they went over the hills and arrived at the place where the
town of San Juan de Castro now stands. They continued their
journey through the valleys known to-day as the San Felipe, in
the immediate vicinity of Hollister. After this they crossed
the Carneadero creek (known at present as Gilroy), ascended
and crossed the small hills of Linares (Lomita de la Linares)
and the dry lake known as the Rancho of Juan Alvirez; went
over the gap of Santa Teresa, and entered the valley of Santa
Clara, where are situated the cities of San José and Santa Clara,
only separated from each other by the Guadalupe river.

"Here," said Father Crespí, "is a magnificent place to found
a Mission, because it possesses all the necessary resources:
abundance of good lands, water, and timber, and a great many
gentiles to baptize." Thence they continued along the eastern
shores of the Bay, arrived at Alameda creek (Alvarado city,
Vallejo's Mills and Centreville), followed along the Bay towards
the north, crossed San Lorenzo creek (Haywards), thence to
San Lorenzo, Oakland, San Pablo, El Pinole, Martinez, Pacheco,
Suisun Bay, and crossed the San Joaquin river, at a point not
far distant from Antioch. This was on the 30th of March.

As the expedition did not possess the means of surmounting
such obstacles as it met and reach Point Reyes, which was its
objective point, it was determined to return to Monterey by a
different route—that is, along the foot-hills of Mount Diablo..
The President of the Missions having become fully convinced
of the impossibility of establishing that of San Francisco immediately at its own port, as he lacked the means of transporta-
tion by sea, and in order to proceed by land, additional explor-

ing parties were deemed necessary. He reported the failure of the expedition of Fages to the Viceroy of New Spain. The Viceroy gave orders to Captain Don Fernando Rivera y Moncada, who had been appointed successor to Fages in command of the Military Posts (Presidios) of New California, to make a second examination, for the purpose of discovering the most appropriate localities for the foundation of the Missions in project. At the same time, in his letters of the 25th of May, he calls upon Father Junípero to aid and assist the new commander and to occupy and establish Missions in the most convenient and suitable places.

Accordingly, having made the necessary preparations, Captain Rivera started from Monterey on the 23d of November, 1774, accompanied by Father Francisco Palou, an escort of sixteen soldiers, and some servants. They prosecuted their journey without having encountered any drawback as far as the valley of Santa Clara; but from there they went to the west of the Bay between its shores and the adjacent hills. Following the level plains in the said valley, they passed by Bay View, Mayfield, the Pulgas, (Menlo Park,) Redwood City, Belmont, San Mateo, San Bruno and Laguna de la Merced, and reached Point Lobos. They crossed the ravines, and ascended the mountain whence they beheld the entrance to the Port of San Francisco, (the Golden Gate). On the 4th of December they planted the symbol of Christianity on the most elevated point close to where now stands the castle or fortification of the National Government, that is, on the southern portion of what forms the mouth of the said harbor; "on account of that being a spot upon which no Spaniard or Christian had yet trod," according to the narrative of Father Palou.

That cross I saw myself, in the year 1829, having come to San Francisco on business pertaining to the military service. No location was at that time made, either for a garrison (Presidio) or Mission, as the severity of the winter months compelled the expedition to return to winter quarters at Monterey; and they verified it by going over the route that was taken by the expedition of 1769, which was by San Pedro, and Spanishtown,

(Half Moon Bay), in the county of San Mateo, Point New Year, Santa Cruz City, Watsonville in Santa Cruz county, Pajaro City, Castroville, Salinas, and Monterey, which had been their starting point.

In the year 1775, during the months of August and September, Captain Ayala entered the Bay of San Francisco, on board the packet-boat *San Carlos*, this being the first historically authenticated vessel that sailed into that bay. He remained forty days and explored it in all directions. Captain Ezeta and Father Palou came up from Monterey as far as the place where Rivera and the same Missionary Father had planted the mentioned cross, but they did not find the crew of the *San Carlos*.

The next attempt to found a religious and military establishment at San Francisco proved successful. The Lieutenant-Colonel, Don Juan Bautista de Anza, by orders from the Viceroy Fray Don Antonio Maria Bucarelli y Ursúa, recruited soldiers and settlers (pobladores) in Sinaloa and gave them all the aid possible to facilitate their journey to their new homes in Upper California. Being all assembled at San Miguel de Orcasitas, (Sonora), they started upon their march on the 29th of September, 1775, by way of the Colorado river, which had already been explored by the same Anza in another expedition. The colony was composed of thirty married soldiers and twelve families of settlers, which, together, formed a total of two hundred souls, who were to found and establish the new towns. Before the departure of this expedition by land in March, 1775, one ship and two packet-boats sailed for San Blas, taking on board provisions and effects for the Missions and Presidios. Providence favored the three vessels, which were successful in their operations. On the 4th of January, 1776, Lieutenant-Colonel Anza arrived at the Mission of San Gabriel with his expedition. Urgent business concerning the security of the establishments in Southern California detained him there. By the 12th of March, he had already reached the Mission of El Carmelo accompanied by the chaplain, Father Pedro Font, and his escort. On the 22d of March, he set out on a journey to examine the region of country of this port of San Francisco, and

arrived at the place where Father **Palou, in** accord with Captain
Rivera, had planted the cross in December, 1774. Having examined the locality well, **Anza and the Lieutenant** Don **José Joaquin** Moraga decided that **a garrison (Presidio) should be
founded** there, **and that this subordinate officer should be the
one to carry the project into execution.**

The expedition continued on their journey; and, according to
Father Palou, upon arriving at the Bay, **which was** called "Las
Lloronas," (the primitive name of Mission **Bay),** they crossed
a creek by which a large lake is **drained, which was called** "De
Los Dolores," and that site **appeared to them as a suitable** spot
for a Mission which **had to be founded in the vicinity of the new
advanced military post (Presidio). They continued on their
journey and went further North than the place where Fages and
Father Crespí had been, and then returned to Monterey.**

On the 17th of June, 1776, the expedition of soldiers and
families from Sonora started from Monterey. The military
force was commanded **by Lieutenant Don José Joaquin** Moraga;
it was composed **of one sergeant, two corporals and ten** or
twelve soldiers, with **their wives and children. There were also,
in the party,** seven **families of resident settlers, five servants,
muleteers and** vaqueros **(stock herders,) who took care of 200**
head **of cattle** belonging **to the King and private individuals.**
This is concerning the new **garrison. In what appertains to** the
Mission, **I will say** that **there were Fathers Francisco** Palou
and Pedro Benito Cambon, **two servants and** three neophyte
Indians, one of whom was from the Mission of San Carlos, and
the two others from Old California, these having 86 head of
cattle in their charge.

The expedition took the same route as that of 1774, and arrived
safely on the 27th of the same month at the Lake of Dolores,
where it had to wait for the packet-boat *San Carlos*, to determine
upon the location of the garrison and fort. Meantime, it occupied
itself in exploring the surrounding country. On the 28th, the
Lieutenant ordered an Euramada, **a hut made of** branches of
trees, to be made, which might **serve as a** chapel for the purpose
of celebrating **Mass; and it was in it** that the first Mass was said,

on the 29th, which was the feast of the glorious apostles Saints Peter and Paul. The Fathers continued celebrating in the same "Euramada," every day until the garrison (Presidio) was established near the landing place, where good water could be obtained and the land was appropriate. I said good water, as subsequent experience proves it to be excellent and possessing some marvelous qualities. In proof of my assertion, I appeal to the testimony of the families of Miramontes, Martinez, Sanchez, Soto, Briones and others, all of whom had wives that bore twins upon several instances; and public opinion attributes, not without reason, these wholesome results to the virtues of the waters of the "Polin," which still exists. The exploration remained a whole month encamped awaiting the arrival of the ship, during which time the soldiers and settlers were busy cutting timber in order to gain time.

The month having expired without the packet-boat making its appearance, the commander, Moraga, determined to make over to the spot which he had in the course of his explorations selected as more appropriate for the new garrison (Presidio). This he did on the 26th of July, and all hands went to work and made barracks out of "Tule," which might serve them as places of shelter. The first barrack that was built was dedicated to serve as a chapel, and the first Mass was celebrated by Father Palou on the 28th. But, by order of Lieutenant Moraga, there remained near the Lake de los Dolores the two missionary priests and servants, with the stock and everything else appertaining to the Mission—all under the immediate protection of six soldiers. The Fathers occupied themselves in building houses, the soldiers of the guard and one resident settler assisting in the work. This was the reason why the Reverend Father Palou certified on the first page of the primitive Books of Baptisms, Marriages and Deaths, that the Mission had been founded on the 1st day of August, 1776.

I beg leave to be permitted here to mention (because it has some connection with part of our history,) that during the month of August Father Palou administered, on the 10th day, the waters of Baptism, *abinstantem mortem*, to a child a few days old, who was the legitimate son of Ignacio **Soto and** Maria Barbara de Lugo, my mother's aunt, **which said child** was called Francisco José de Los Dolores; and **on the** 25th day a little girl 15 **days** old, the legitimate **daughter of José** Antonio **Sanchez and Maria** de Los Dolores **Morales, was baptized and called** Juana Maria **Lorenza. This child was taken to the baptismal** font **of** the **Mission by Don José Canizares, pilot of the packet-boat** San Carlos.

The long looked-for San Carlos entered the **Port of** San Francisco and anchored at twelve o'clock, **A. M.**, on the 18th of August, opposite the encampment where **the** garrison had to be **erected.** Captain **Quirós, his pilots, and** the chaplain (Father **Nocedal) went** immediately **on shore. After the customary salutation had passed, they inspected the land selected by Moraga for a garrison, as well as that of the Mission, and it was agreed that both places were** suitable for the purposes to which **they** had **been destined. According to the very words used by** the **Reverend Father Palou, in his diary of the expedition,** which reads: **"About the middle of September, 1776, the soldiers had already built their wooden houses, all duly roofed; the Lieutenant had his royal house, and a warehouse made of the same material had** been **completed of sufficient capacity to contain all the supplies that the vessel had brought. It was immediately** decided **that the festival should be celebrated with a** solemn procession, **fixing** upon the day as **that of the** 17th of September, **the same on which Our** Mother the **Church celebrates the** memory **of the Impression of the** Wounds **of our Seraphic Father** Saint **Francis. The day could not have been more** appropriate, as it **was that of the Patron Saint of the Port, of the new garrison (Presidio,) and of the** Mission.''

And for taking possession of the Mission was fixed the 4th day of *October,* which is the *very* day of *our* Seraphic Father, Saint *Francis.''*[*]

---

[*] My assertions concerning the day of the Foundation having been more than once controverted, I here take occasion to explain my position on that point. The Rev. Father Palou, it is true, states that, on account of Lieut. Moraga **not having** returned from his expedition, the ceremonies,

*5

The ceremony of the solemn possession and foundation of the Mission took place on the 4th of October. The Lieutenant, Don José Joaquin Moraga and his soldiers, Don Fernando Quiros, commander of the packet-boat, his two pilots, the major part of his crew, and, lastly, the never-forgotten Fathers Palou, Tomas de la Péna, Cambon, and Nocedal, were present. I will quote from Father Palou again: "A solemn mass was sung by the Fathers; the ceremony of the formal possession was made by the Royal officers, and when it had been completed all went into the church and sang a *Te Deum Laudamus*, with the ringing of bells, and, at times, firing salutes with cannon and other fire-arms, the ship responding with its artillery."

It is not only the diary of Father Palou that serves me as authority to fix upon with exactness the day of the possession and foundation respectively of the garrison and Mission. These data I had obtained a long time before I had seen and read the said diary from the lips of the same military men and settlers

---

which were to be held at the Mission on the 4th, were suspended or postponed, after Mass was celebrated, and that the Lieutenant having arrived on the 7th, the Celebration of the Foundation took place on the following day, the 8th of October. In the "*Life of Father Junipero Serra*," by the same author, mention is made in the book, which is verified by official documents, that the celebration took place on *the ninth* (9th) of October. These dates are given in figures, and they may possibly be typographical errors in one or both of the cases quoted. Be that as it may, it is beyond question that the old Fathers, since my earliest recollection—and, from tradition, I know, before my time—always considered the *fourth* of *October*, the Feast of the Patron Saint, as the date of the Foundation, and celebrated the anniversaries on that day in accordance with their belief. It may be urged that the celebration of the 4th of October was actually that of the Patron Saint ; but would not this rather tend to strengthen my assertion that, having selected a Patron for their Mission, they would *dedicate that day to the celebration* of the foundation? I do not wish to be at variance with the gentlemen who differ with me on those points ; but I owe it to myself to maintain what of my own knowledge has been the accepted opinion of those who have long since passed away. The fact of the postponement of the celebration of an event from accidental causes will not change the original intention. The celebration of the anniversary of American Independence, when the 4th of July falls on Sunday, is always held on the Monday following ; but it is the *celebration of the Fourth of July*, nevertheless. M. G. VALLEJO.

who were eye-witnesses to those ceremonies; that is to say, from Lieutenant Moraga, from my father, **Don Ygnacio** Vallejo, Don Marcos Briones, Galindo, Castro, **Pacheco,** Bojorques, Bernal, Higuera, Peralta, **Amézquita, Franco Flores,** Hernandez, **Mesa and others whose names I do not here enumerate, as I do not wish to be too lengthy.**

The temporary building of the church was situated at a distance of about one thousand varas to the northwest of the spot where the actual Temple now stands. The Lake of Dolores was at the time located and could be seen to the right of the road coming from the Presidio to the Mission between two hills, one of which still exists, the other one has disappeared before the progressive march of this rich emporium.

On the 8th day of October, of the mentioned year 1776, the erection of the present temple of the Mission of San Francisco was commenced, and we to-day on this centennial anniversary, have met here, not only to honor the memory of those who dedicated it to the service of God, but also to show our admiration of the great principles, by which they were impelled, namely, the faith of Him who died nailed on the cross for the redemption of man.

Providence, which is infinitely wise and bountiful, has permitted that our venerable pastor should make mention of my father's being one of those brave men who aided and assisted the Missionaries with his sword. Consequently, at the same time that I satisfy your desires, I comply with a duty very satisfactory to myself in being the exponent of events that transpired one hundred years ago, the date upon which commenced the life and existence of San Francisco, which we can with pride style the Queen City of the Pacific. *Justitæ soror fides*—Faith is the sister of Justice. I shall be guided in my remarks by a pure and holy love for these two sisters. The invigorating breath of the gospel, as I said before, was given to us by some Franciscan Friars, who were indeed poor and humble Missionaries of God, but rich in Faith and Hope in the success of their grand and arduous task. By this means were sown the prolific seeds of Christianity that has given such marvelous results

during the one hundred years of its existence, which this rich and
populous city counts; having written it to-day the Metropolitan
Church, and which, by circumstances and coincidences that would
be too lengthy to narrate, bears also the name of San Francisco.
The Metropolitan Church, I said. Yes, it is the one over which
our worthy Archbishop Alemany so honorably presides.

Let us for a moment transport ourselves from this day to the
former century, and let us compare the present gathering here to
an assemblage of that epoch. The latter consisted of a handful
of men who were brave Christians, armed to the teeth, and of
another still smaller party of humble ministers of Christ, but
gifted with wondrous fortitude and a firm determination that
nothing could change or oppose, as they had come to preach the
Word of God and were resigned to take upon themselves the
crown of martyrdom. Both of these parties were liable to become at any moment the victims of a rude crowd of naked
savage gentiles, some of whom had come to them at first through
curiosity, others prompted by a spirit of destruction, and all of
them anxious to obtain the presents which were given to them for
the purpose of alluring them and inspiring them with confidence
and have them hear for the first time the words of the Gospel.

The audience whom I have the honor to address on this occasion is a true representative of the high culture and advanced
civilization of the nineteenth century, enjoying all the security
and privileges which that state of society guarantees to them.

What a vast difference, gentlemen, between what was, and what
we see to-day, in this centennial which we celebrate ! Let us
bear in mind that in the course only of one hundred years, this
privileged place has taken a gigantic stride and fallen into the
hands of a society worthy of prosecuting the work that was begun
by those true Pioneers. The Mission of San Francisco, which at
one time was situated on a desert, yet protected by the hand of
Providence, to-day may be seen nearly in the centre of this populous city of the same name.

The foundation of the Mission and military post (Presidio)
having been completed, the packet-boat sailed on the 21st, for
San Blas. During its stay in the Port the Commander (Quirós)

had lent all the aid possible **to the** Mission in getting a carpenter and some sailors help to in **the** construction of doors and windows for the church and house **of the** missionary Fathers, **also in** the building **of the** altar, **as well as in many other things.** Not satisfied with all this, Captain Quirós left **four of his crew to work as day laborers on the buildings that were being erected and in the tilling of the ground, which was** immediately commenced.

I remember this, together with other things, **that I** heard in my **youth** from the eye-witnesses of these transactions. Among them **I** should mention the boatswain **of the packet-boat** known **by everybody as** Neustramo **Pepe. This brave man, who was a Catalonian by birth, had a heart as sensitive as a woman's.** He visited **my father's house at Monterey a great many times in after years, and in conversations** had **with our family he often related** the fact of **the foundation of the Post and** Mission of San **Francisco, where** he had worked with an energy worthy of all **praise.** A great many times and on several occasions he said to my **father, shedding tears:** " **Do you** remember, Don **Ygnacio,** our farewell **on board of the packet-boat when Captain** Quirós **gave** the banquet **to** the officers **and priests? Do you recollect how afterwards the** military and **naval** officers, with **the priests, who were** assembled at the landing **place** on the beach, **embraced** one another **and** shook **hands? Do** you remember that from **there,** after **we weighed anchor, all the** military men and the priests went towards the strip of land that projects out and forms **the southern cape** of the Port (where now stands the fortification), **and** while they were there they **waved their** handkerchiefs and their hats **to us as we** passed, **kindly** bidding us a last **adieu?** What a solemn day was that, my friend! Do you remember how the currents dragged our vessel towards the opposite shores **of the** harbor; and how **we** were there exposed to great danger, **until a favorable** breeze came up from the northwest, and **saved** us **from** being dashed against the cliffs of rocks? Yet, in the midst of that tribulation, and such despair, we left in sorrow for you who remained exposed, and at the mercy of so many barbarians. **Why,** man, even Quirós shed tears!''

Before leaving our friend, Nuestramo **Pepe**, it is very gratifying to me to mention that his popularity among our people was so great, that no sooner would there be news of the arrival of some ship on the coast—that is, at San Diego or some other inhabited place—than every one would inquire whether Nuestramo Pepe had come; and if he was there he would be received with enthusiastic hurrahs and cries of acclamation by all the people present.

We already have our apostolic men engaged in the great work of the redemption of thousands of gentiles to whom God had opened the way to heaven. It seems to me that I see those intrepid men (ministers of the altar and warriors of shield and sword,) in these regions, surrounded by a ferocious and barbarous people whom they had to conquer for God and their sovereign. Combining the two expedients, which affects the human heart most? The main object which both priests and soldiers had in view had to be attained. "*Suaviter in modo, fortiter in re.*" The mildness of the minister of God upheld by the force of armed men produced the desired effects.

The assiduity of the missionaries never relaxed before the numerous obstacles daily thrown in their way. With the meekness of true Apostles, they succeeded in getting the barbarians to present themselves voluntarily to receive the waters of baptism. By holy abnegation, the example of their virtues, and of their constancy, they at last gained the confidence of a considerable number of catechumens who gradually began to draw near.

It is a fact known by all the Californians, old as well as new, that whole tribes from the surroundings of the Bay came to accept a religious faith, which, till then, had been wholly unknown to them; but, for all that, there were some turbulent, wicked ones who from the commencement had been opposed to the advancement or progress of the *foreigners*, as they called the Spaniards in their own dialect. This feeling of animosity was made evident a few days later when the *Buriburi* from the Indian Villages (rancherias) afterwards called San Mateo, attacked one hut situated about three miles from the Laguna de Los Dolores and set it on fire. Such was the terror which this act

caused in them, that **not even the** assurance of protection which
was promised them by the garrison was sufficient **to** prevent
their crossing on their tule rafts to the opposite side of the peninsula, which **to-day is Marin county,** as well to that **on the** East,
which is known at present as Oakland, **Alameda,** etc. **The fu-
gitives kept away for some time ; but at last they commenced to
visit the Presidio, and, by December, became so** courageous, that
they considered themselves strong enough to commit depreda-
tions on the Mission.

The commanding-sergeant of the guard, Juan Pablo **Grijalva,**
caused one of those who had been hostile **to be** flogged, **and this
act alarmed and enraged the friends of the** culprit. **Two of
them fired** their **arrows at the soldiers, but luckily did not do
any harm. On the following day the sergeant determined to
chastise the audacity of those who had been turbulent, after
which an encounter took place with them in which one of
the** residents **was** wounded who killed his **antagonist with** one
shot, and his body fell into the estuary. The rest of the **Indians
fled, but went to some rocks from whence they continued their**
hostilities.

A shot well aimed **by the sergeant struck one of the gentiles**
in the thigh, **the ball going through and** lodging **in the rocks,**
from **where** it was **taken by the Indians.** The death of **one and**
the wounding **of another of the savages discouraged them to**
such a degree that **they asked for peace, which** the sergeant
granted to them. Nevertheless, **the two** Indians who had been
the cause of the encounter were taken prisoners. The sergeant
had them chastised severely, giving them to understand that if,
in the future, they again manifested hostility they should forfeit
their lives. This unfortunate occurrence retarded somewhat the
conversion of those gentiles for **several** months; **but about the
beginning of 1777 they could be seen** about the Mission, and
three of them were baptised on the 29th **of June of that year.**

On the 6th of January, 1777, a party of armed **soldiers, under
the command of Lieutenant** Moraga, with an escort, and Father
Tomas de la Peña, went from San Francisco to the place where
the Mission of Santa Clara was founded; and another came later,

accompanying Father José Murguia, from San Carlos or the Carmelo, bringing provisions and supplies for that same place. Both priests were to remain in charge of the new establishment. Father Murguia did not arrive until the 21st, but Father Peña had already celebrated Mass there on the 12th.

The work of the missionaries continued without interruption on the part of the Indians. In 1778, the ship *Santiago*, alias *Nueva Galicia*, arrived from San Blas, bringing on board a cargo of provisions for the Mission of San Francisco, together with other effects and merchandise for the Presidio. Nothing worthy of mention occurred until the latter part of June, 1779, on which date the ship *Santiago* entered the Port of San Francisco again with supplies and merchandise for the Mission and Presidio. In the year 1780 the vessel *Santiago* did not visit the Port of San Francisco, but left at Monterey one hundred fanegas (Spanish bushels) of corn and other merchandise which it became necessary to transport by land with very great difficulty. Worse was the fate not only of San Francisco, but of all the Missions and garrisons (Presidios) of Northern California in 1781, as no provisions or yearly supplies from the King arrived. This caused great inconvenience, and did considerable damage to the conquest.

Our virtuous missionaries had in that year already reaped such abundant fruits from the vineyard, which they were cultivating for our Lord Jesus Christ, that the Reverend Father-President Junípero Serra, came to San Francisco for the first time, and, exercising the powers with which he had been vested by the Holy See, administered the sacrament of Confirmation to 69 neophytes.

The following year of 1782 was also unfortunate on account of the great loss suffered by the Missions in the death of the old missionary Father, Friar Juan Crespí. This venerable man and wise apostle had already counted thirty years of missionary life among the Indians, and came to New California in the expedition that founded the first establishment at San Diego, in the year 1769. In the next succeeding year, he was present at the foundation of the Mission of San Carlos de Monterey. I have

THE FIRST SHIP ENTERING THE GOLDEN GATE.

already related the **active** part which he **took with** the Commander Fages in trying to **find** a place suitable for the establishment of another Mission at **the Port** of San Francisco. **These** eminent and invaluable services **which** he rendered entitle him to the highest position **among the many worthy missionaries of his Seraphic Order.**

On **the 13th of May, 1783, two vessels** entered our ports with **supplies and** provisions **for the** Presidios and Missions that had **already been** founded. Friar Pedro Benito Cambon, **who** had **been** absent on several occasions, was sent back to this Mission to accompany Father Palou.

On **the** mentioned date, **two other vessels arrived with more provisions and merchandise,** bringing **an auxiliary force of** missionaries, **composed of the Reverend Fathers, Friar Juan** Antonio Garcia **Rioboo, and Friar Diego Nobóa. Both of** these **clergymen remained in the Mission** of San Francisco, and took part with **the** resident ministers in celebrating the feast of *Corpus Christi* with **all the** solemnity that their means allowed.

After this they were **called** away by the President and ordered to go **to Monterey. The missionary Fathers, at the same time** that they worked for **the good of the soul, did not neglect** material happiness.

When they **had a pretty large congregation of** converts under subjection, they dedicated them **to works of industry.** Besides the agricultural pursuits, from which the missionaries as well as **the** neophytes and catechumens were to receive their subsistence, **adobes, bricks, tiles, etc.,** were made, **and the** construction of the **holy temple was** begun; granaries, residences, quarters and a guard-house for **the** soldiers, and **lastly,** houses for those Indians **who** had been converted to Christianity, were built. It will be readily seen by this account that the most worthy Fathers were **constantly** employed in their spiritual as well as temporal labors: although **the** latter was always subordinate to the former.

In one of **my journeys to** San Francisco, during the year 1826, I found this Mission in all its splendor and state of preservation, consisting, at that **time, of one church,** the residence of the Rev. Fathers, granaries, **warehouses for** merchandise, guard-house for the soldiers, prison, an orchard of fruit trees and vegetable garden, cemetery, the entire rancheria (Indian village) all constructed of adobe houses with tile roofs—the whole laid out with great regularity, forming streets, and a tannery and soap factory—that is to say, on that portion which actually lies between Church, Dolores and Guerrero streets, from north to south, and between Fifteenth and Seventeenth streets, from east to west. I think that the neophytes living in the Mission, in San Mateo, and in San Pedro reached six hundred souls.

In the year 1830, I was directed by my superior officer to continue to serve at the Presidios. Everything was in the same state of preservation in which I had left it in 1826.

I recollect, with joy, that on the 4th of October, 1830, while the Reverend Father Friar Thomas Estenega was minister of the Mission, and I was acting as adjutant of the garrison (Presidio), the military commander was invited to take part with his officers in the celebration; consequently, all the soldiers were present that he who now addresses you had under his orders. Salutes were fired in front of the church and residence of the priests on that day in regular order. There were also present at the celebration of the holy Patron Saint, the Reverend Fathers, Friar José Viader of the Mission of Santa Clara, Friar Buenaventura Fortuni, of that of San Francisco Solano, and Friar Juan Amorós, of that of San Rafael. During the Mass, the last priest mentioned officiated, while Fathers Viader and Fortuni acted as deacon and sub-deacon—Father Estenega (who was still young) being left in charge of the choir, music, etc.

A sermon was preached by Father Viader, relating to the festivity of the holy Patron, and to the foundation of the place on the 4th of October, 1776.

This was the last celebration at which four Spanish priests, from Spain, assisted with the same object as that had by the meritorious Pioneers, and the ministers Palou, Cambon, Peña, and Nocedal on the 4th of October, 1776, *one hundred years ago*. What a singular coincidence! I will give a short biography of those apostolic men.

Reverend Friar José Viader **was a man of refined manners;** tall in stature, somewhat severe in his aspect, open **and frank in** his conversation. He was as austere in religious matters as he was active in **the management of** the temporalities of **the Mission of** .Santa Clara, **which he always administered.** He became **remarkable among other things, because the Rosary, which he** carried **fastened to the girdle of the Order around** his waist, **had a large crucifix attached to it.**

Friar Fortuni was a holy man who **was** incessantly praying; he could always be seen in or out of the Mission with the Bre-viary in his hand, or reciting the **Rosary in** the church : he **was very learned and affable in his intercourse** with the people **of** those times; and was **very humble, and, besides,** a great apostle.

Friar **Tomas Estenega was a young man of medium height, the personification of activity, of jovial disposition, select and varied in his conversation,** an excellent and very sincere priest. **He** had seen a great deal **of the war of** Revolution in Spain, and was there during **the** French invasion, when Napoleon I. and **his brother Joseph tried** to appropriate to themselves that privileged **land.**

Friar Juan Amorós **was sanctity itself ; and if I possessed the** eloquence **of the great orators, I would consume more time in** depicting the **brilliant** qualities **which** adorned that venerable missionary. **But not** having those talents I shall limit my remarks, and say that Father Amorós was **a model of** virtue, **charity,** humility, and of Christian meekness—a man without a **blemish, of a** candid heart, and of most exemplary life ; he was **the admiration of his** contemporaries **and the** astonishment of the tribes of the aborigines.

When I was a child, nearly seventy years ago, **I knew him at the** Mission of San Carlos of Monterey as chaplain **of the gar-rison of the same name.** When he came to celebrate **Mass in** the chapel **of the** soldiers on Sundays he **always** brought a few sweet figs, dates **and raisins in the sleeve of his habit,** which he distributed after Mass to the boys of the Sunday school; but **this he did after he had given instruction in Christian** Doctrine for half an hour.   On the 14th of July, 1832, this apostolic missionary died at the Mission of San Rafael, at half-past three o'clock in the morning.

The register of his burial says that he was a native of the Province of Catalonia (Spain), born on the 10th October, 1773; took the habit of Our Seraphic Father San Francisco on the 28th of April, 1791; was admitted into the Order by making the necessary vows on the 30th of the same month of the following year, and was ordained priest in the month of December, 1797. On the 4th of March, 1803, he left Catalonia to come to the College of San Fernando, in the city of Mexico, where he arrived on the 26th of July.

In 1804, animated by his great zeal for the conversion of the gentiles, with the blessing of his superiors, he came to the missions of Upper California, where he arrived in the commencement of the year 1804, and was appointed as minister to the Mission of San Carlos, where he lived fifteen years, acting as resident apostolic minister.   From there, by permission of his superior, who was the Reverend Father Prefect, Friar Mariano Payeras, he went to that of San Rafael, where he worked and labored with astonishing perseverance until his death.   He was buried in the Mission church on the 4th of July, at five o'clock in the afternoon.

I must remark that the Mission of San Rafael was for several years a branch of that of San Francisco, and always remained under the jurisdiction of this Presidio.   I speak with so much feeling of kindness towards Father Amorós, because I am cognizant of his great virtues, his pure heart and sincere devotion. Moreover, it was with him that I made my first Confession; and from his holy hands I received for the first time the consecrated bread of the Eucharist.

I have already made mention of his moral gifts, it remains now for me only to describe his physical aspect; and I could not give you a more exact idea of him, nor draw a more perfect likeness from the original, than by calling your attention to the person of a most esteemed ecclesiastic who is here present; his stature, manners, features, smile and amiable disposition all

bring back to my memory the image of that holy man. Neither
Rulofson nor any other of our most skilled photographers could
produce as perfect a picture of Father Amorós than that
which we have before us in the person of our venerable Archbishop, Joseph Sadoc Alemany. And, at the same time, I feel
highly pleased to say, that it is not only in the physical qualities
that I find a great resemblance in the two men.

I must observe here, that during the first years of the Foundation, as the Indians of the Buriburi tribe were not willing to live
in this place on account of it being extremely cold and destitute
of those fine groves of trees which the hand of Providence was
pleased to plant in the region which they occupied, and as the
Indians from San Pedro were enjoying the benefits of their
fertile lands, and hence opposed to come and live in a climate so
different from that in which they were born, in order to remedy
this inconvenience, and at the same time avail themselves of religious instruction, both tribes petitioned the Father ministers,
asking to be allowed to live on their lands, obligating themselves
to build chapels and to dedicate themselves to agricultural pursuits and other labors, all of which was done with great success.

The priests went every Saturday, accompanied by an escort,
said mass, preached, and then returned to the mother church.
The ministers maintained for some time a chapel and store-
houses for grain amongst the Juchiyunes, Acalanes, Bolgones
and Carquinez Indians, who occupied that portion of country
known as Contra Costa. The chapel was located in what is
known to-day as the rancho of San Pablo, where the missionaries
went to comply with their ministerial duties, and, besides, to
direct the works and attend to the administration of their temporalities.

The immense wealth of the Mission of San Francisco was acquired from those three farms, and from its own lands, which
were situated from Rincon Point to Hayes Valley (El Gentil),
Devisadero, and the Garrison (Presidio) to Point Lobos. These
were recognized as its boundaries, from the time of the ancient
founders; upon which grazed all its cattle, horses, sheep and
hogs, and from which abundant crops of wheat, corn and beans
were harvested.

The foundation of San Rafael was made on the 14th of December, 1817. High Mass was celebrated by the Rev. Prefect, Father Vicente Francisco de Sarria, assisted by Fathers Luis Gil, Ramon Abella and Narciso Duran, with sermon and other ceremonies analogous to the occasion. Father Serria baptised four little Indians, and called them respectively by the names of Rafael, Miguel and Gabriel (in honor of the three Archangels), and the fourth by his own name, Vicente Francisco. Father Louis Gil de Taboda remained as resident priest there.

This Mission was the fourth daughter of that of San Francisco; the first having been that of Santa Clara, as I have already said, the second that of Santa Cruz, which was founded on the 29th of August 1791, and the third was that of San José founded on the 11th of June, 1797. The last one was that of San Francisco Solano (Sonoma Valley), founded in 1823 ; abandoned soon after on account of the incursions of the Indians, and reëstablished in 1827, under the supervision of the virtuous Father Fortuni ; but it was not rebuilt permanently until 1830.

The Spanish successors of the worthy Fathers Palou and Cambon in this Mission were, if my memory serves me right, Friars Ramon Abella, Juan Lucio, Juan Cabot, José Altimira and Tomas Estenega. I was personally acquainted with all of them, and I can testify to their being worthy ministers of God and indefatigable apostles.

And now, permit me to make a few remarks in defense of the good name of some of the individuals who governed this country during the Mexican Administration, whose reputation has been sometimes wantonly attacked; while nothing has ever been said against the Governors, under Spain, who preceded them.

Much has been said, and even more has been written, concerning the Missions and their great wealth. And who are they that figure in that drama? Who are its authors? Are they, perchance, impartial men? or, to say the least, have they an accurate knowledge of the history of the Missions of this Upper California? No, no! gentlemen; they were foreign writers, interested parties, and consequently partial in their style; who, without reflection, hurriedly advanced, as undeniable fact, that which was false, all for the purpose of deluding the ignorant and of profiting by the utterance of base falsehoods, at the same time that they flattered their taste by censuring indirectly and unfairly the acts of the collectors of the Missions, styling them thieves, etc. That the Missions were rich we all know. But what were those riches ? This they do not tell us. Nevertheless, these riches consisted in moveable stock and agricultural productions; but they make no mention of pecuniary wealth.

That the Mexican Governors robbed the Missions is an absurdity. The first Mexican Governor, Don Luis A. Argüello, a native of San Francisco, was decidedly a protector of the Missions and a friend to the Missionaries. He died poor, leaving to his family no other patrimony than the small rancho of Las Pulgas, with a few head of stock.

The second Governor, Don José Maria de Echeandia, exercised his authority in the time of the Republic; and although he was always directly opposed to the Spanish priests because they would not swear to the Mexican Constitution, nevertheless, he extended to them his protection as much as it was in his power, and in conformity with the instructions which he had from the new Government. From this resulted, necessarily, a misunderstanding between the ancient ministers and the New Governor, who esteemed them highly; and if he had to act against some of them, it was done for a legal cause, and not because he had any antipathy or hatred towards them.

After having governed the country for five years, Echeandia had great difficulty in collecting and getting together, by the aid of the priests of San Luis Rey and San Juan Capistrano, who were his friends, the sum of three thousand dollars which he needed to return to Mexico. Don Manuel Victoria was the third Governor, who, from his coming into power, gained the good will of the missionaries and was always upon the best terms with them. All the steps towards secularization which had been taken by his predecessor were annulled by Victoria, even before he was in possession of the Government. His official conduct was despotic, and he forced the Californians to send him out of the country; yet it would be an injustice to accuse him of having robbed either the country or the Missions. The priests aided him pecuniarily, that he might be able to leave.

Don José Figueroa, the fourth Mexican Governor, was an educated and upright man. He died poor at Monterey.

Castro, Gutierrez, Chico, Alvarado, Micheltorena, and, lastly, Pio Pico, all had to contend with revolutionary elements. The priests had disappeared, the neophytes had left the Missions and gone away to the villages of the gentiles, and the government, under such circumstances, had to take possession of the lands which were claimed by the Missions, through the power which it possessed, and in order to defend the country against an *invasion with which it was threatened*.

When the old missionaries saw that the political tornado was about to burst upon the Mission system, they commenced to convert into money all their moveable property, such as cattle and stock. In the Missions of San Gabriel, San Fernando, San Juan Capistrano and San Luis Rey, they killed by contract with private individuals, during the years 1830, 1831 and 1832, more than sixty thousand head of cattle, from which they only saved the hides. The pecuniary wealth of the Missions in their primitive days, which were more productive, was sent out of the country to Spain, Mexico or Italy. This I know, and presume, and even believe, that all of it arrived safely at its place of destination. Be that as it may, neither the Governors nor the Californians ever partook of any of that wealth, with the exception of $20,000, which, upon an occasion of imperative necessity, we, the members of the Deputation, together with other prominent citizens, obtained from Father José Sanchez of the Mission of San Gabriel, to facilitate the payment of the expenses of a military force destitute of everything at the time, thus avoiding the commission of greater evils.

During the lengthy period of the war of Independence, and even afterwards, the Missions supplied the troops of the Cuera (leather coats) with provisions and other effects, as no more yearly supplies had been sent from Mexico.

But it is necessary to bear in mind that the Spanish flag waved over California, and that the priests did no more than comply with the orders of the King, at the same time that they looked for their own protection and that of the Missions, soldiers being constantly engaged in protecting the Missions, and in continuous campaigns for the purpose of keeping the Indians under subjection. Without those soldiers, the Indians would have risen immediately against the Missions, and all the white inhabitants would have inevitably perished.

The missionaries from the College of our Lady of Guadalupe, Zacatecas, came from Mexico in the year 1832, and it was the lot of the Mission of San Francisco to have, as a missionary Father José Maria Gutierrez, who continued here for some time. After that, Fathers Lorenzo Guijas and Mercado had charge of it alternately. When this Mission was secularized it was delivered over to several overseers (mayordomos) who were appointed by the Political Government, until the Indian priest, Prudencio Santillan, took charge of it. This Rev. Father had been ordained in sacris by the first Bishop in California, Friar Don Francisco Garcia Diego.

I have occupied the attention of this intelligent audience so long for the purpose of giving a detailed narration of the primitive history of the Presidio, Mission and Pueblo of San Francisco, which up to the year 1846 did not count a population any greater than that within this fine hall—a weak fortification, one or two officers, a company of soldiers and a handful of resident settlers in twenty-five or thirty houses.

What a change is presented to our view to-day! A great city, which, having absorbed the three points mentioned, has filled the entire peninsula with a population of nearly three hundred thousand inhabitants, dedicated to all the arts known to the highest degree of civilization. The harbor and city, protected by strong fortifications and well-equipped ships of war, situated on the most advantageous position, it is destined to become the grand commercial centre of India, China and Japan, at the same time that it will be such for the entire northern coast of the Pacific. What shall be the destiny which the Supreme Benefactor

6

has prepared for this portion of our beautiful native land for the next coming *hundred years?* I entertain the full conviction that the hand of the Great Creator, by which is guided the progress and happiness of mankind, will carry us to the highest degree of excellence in all the branches of knowledge. Then, it is to be hoped, that those who will celebrate that day, taking a retrospective view of the present epoch, will remember with gratitude what this generation, by divine aid, has established for them, to carry on, until they reach moral, intellectual and physical perfection.

And let us from this moment send cordial salutations to our fortunate descendants who will see the brilliant dawn of the second Centennial of the *Foundation of the Mission of San Francisco de Asis.*

At the conclusion of the exercises at the Mechanics' Pavilion, his Grace the Most Rev. Archbishop Alemany and the Right Rev. Bishop O'Connell, escorted by the Grand Marshal's Aids, proceeded in carriages to the Mission Dolores to lay the cornerstone of the new church, which it has been determined to erect on what may indeed be truly styled, in the language of Byron, "haunted, holy ground." The site of the contemplated structure is on the north side of the old Mission church. A block of Rocklin granite, 2 feet by 10 long, 2 feet by $5\frac{1}{2}$ feet broad, and one by seven deep, forms the northern corner of the tower to be erected in connection with the new place of worship. The edifice will be cruciform, of brick, with stone facings and trimmings. On the exposed side of the corner-stone there are simply carved figures of "1876" and a cross. The architect is Mr. P. Huerne, and the estimated cost of the church will be from $80,000 to $90,000. Mr. Edward Connolly is the master-mason and contractor. It will have a frontage of 85 feet. A contribution has already been made to the building fund. Late as it was in the afternoon when the ceremonies of the dedication commenced, a large assemblage was present. The procession was marshaled by Mr. D. J. Oliver. His Grace the Most Rev. Archbishop, attended by the Right Rev. Bishop O'Connell, and the Rev. Father Hugh P. Gallagher, the representative of the Right Rev. Bishop Amat, of Monterey and Los Angeles, and members of the secular and regular clergy of the province of San Francisco, proceeded with the dedication. In front one of the acolytes bore a large crucifix, and tapers were carried by the others. After lowering the stone into position, the Archbishop sprinkled holy water and blessed the site of the contemplated religious edifice. His Grace then placed a metal casket into the cavity of the granite which was closed by marble slabs. He then tapped the stone four times, declared it well laid, and bestowed his benediction. The contents of the casket consisted of a ground-plan of the proposed edifice, a Latin scroll written on vellum, containing a brief mention of the date and facts of the Centennial Celebration, and the purpose for which the building was designed. It was added that the reigning Sovereign Pontiff, Pius IX., was in the thirty-first year of his Pontificate; that Ulyses S. Grant was President of the United States; that William Irwin was Governor of California; that the church, under the invocation of God, was dedicated to St. Francis de Asis; and that the corner-stone was laid by Archbishop Alemany, assisted by Bishop O'Connell and the clergy. Copies of the San Francisco *Monitor and Guardian*, the New York *Freeman's Journal*, the London *Tablet*, and local daily journals, as well as a rare Japanese coin, a half-dollar forty-six years old, and a piece of wood one hundred years old taken from the roof of the old Mission church, were also inclosed in the casket.

Thus terminated, with befitting solemnity, the Centennial Celebration of the founding of the Presidio of San Francisco and the Mission Dolores. That the Commemoration of the chiefest event in the annals of California was a success, cannot be questioned. Nor, apart from the surpassing grandeur of the religious demonstration, and the pomp of martial pageantry, were the civic accessories unworthy of the scene. With the dawn of the anniversary an era of generous feeling seemed to have set in. In the celebration of the memorable day the citizens of the State, headed by his Excellency the Governor and the representatives of Federal authority, participated with hearty good-will. The American colors, carried in a line of some six thousand men, with the Irish and Mexican flags, symbolized a veritable Pacific Union. It took more than an hour for the array to pass a given point. A pleasing feature of the parade were the little girls, dressed in white belonging to the Mission Dolores Sunday School, under the protection of the good Sisters of Notre Dame; and the young ladies of St. Joseph's Sunday School, with crowns of flowers, and white veils.

The students, too, of the Colleges conducted by the Brothers of the Christian Schools, attired in modest regalia, challenged favorable notice. It only remains to add, in the words of an impartial observer in the local daily press, that "such was the order maintained, not a single accident occurred by reason of the crowded condition of the streets and sidewalks; and not a single unpleasant incident was noticed to mar the harmony of the occasion." And as the purple mist which had covered, like a veil, the glory of the morning dissolved in the golden air, and the clouds—"pavilions of the sun," as Bulwer Lytton has it—passed away, the scene was assuredly a brilliant one. Bright with varied hues the stately procession pursued its triumphal march beneath the glance of beautiful eyes moist with emotion, and amid the cheers of the multitude that thronged the sidewalks. Proudly eminent the Stars and Stripes borne by each organization in the line (and which had erewhile floated from many a fortress in New Spain) seemed to derive fresh lustre from the gaudy standards of the Sister Republic, carried by the Mexican Companies. In friendly union with the banners of both countries, blazed, on a field of emerald green, the Harp and Sunburst of Erin, the ally of Catholic Spain in the past and of the Great Republic, from the dawn of National Independence, to our own time. In the First Division, led by Major P. R. O'Brien, were the First Battalion of Cavalry, Second Brigade of the National Guard of California, and the Jackson Dragoons, corps conspicuous as dashing *sabreurs*. It was worthy of note that the Third Regiment of Infantry, under the command of the gallant veteran, Colonel A. Wason, turned out with full ranks. The martial bearing and admirable discipline of the men reflected honor on the State Militia. Foremost, too, among the civic organizations appeared in full strength the Ancient Order of Hibernians with green regalia set off by gold and silver embroidery, whose ranks were reinforced by strong delegations from the neighboring counties. A not unfriendly rivalry seemed to animate the Mexican and Spanish elements of the Third Division. For once, at least, the hostile feeling incident to the revolution that overthrew the domination of Spain in her richest Colonial dependency, not to mention the international difficulties that subsequently disturbed the relations of the two countries, had apparently vanished ; and upon an occasion that appealed to olden memories and the sanctity of a common faith, the Mexican citizen and the Spanish-born subject were united in fraternal effort. Something like the same good-will, if unhappily rare in Spanish America, has always existed among the Catholic families worthy of the name, of Old and New France, and (in a less degree, certainly) of the Catholic manor-houses of Great Britain and the State of Maryland. Mexico, to be sure—the prey of Red-Radicalism and miscreants in power—can hardly be compared with Lower Canada, ever loyal to the Holy See, or with the Catholic colony founded by Lord Baltimore, still true—*per tot discrimina rerum*—to its Conservative traditions, and one of whose sons, the distinguished jurist,

A. H. Loughborough, is one of the most loved and honored representatives of Catholic interests in California. A true Catholic, indeed, would justly ascribe this sudden *entente cordiale* between factions so long and bitterly opposed, to the patronage of the Mother of God—*Reina y Madre de misericordia, vida, dulzura y esperanza nuestra*—under whose standard marched the congregation of the church of our Lady of Guadalupe, escorted by the Juarez Guard, (so called after a late President of Mexico, of unmixed Indian blood), and a well-equipped troop of Spanish gentlemen, not a few of whom were subjects of the Crown of Spain and the Indies. In this connection a faithful chronicler of the Centennial Celebration cannot omit to notice, however briefly and inadequately, the fine appearance presented by the Sodalities of the Blessed Virgin of the church of St. Ignatius—organizations that shed honor upon the zeal of the Jesuit Fathers and the piety of the lay members. Not inferior in living interest, too, were the St. Joseph's Temperance Society, also followers of Mary, the Catholic Temperance Society of St. Bridget's, the Society of St .John the Baptist, and the Cadets of St. Patrick. In the procession, also, were represented the clergy and parishioners of the churches of St. Peter, St. Joseph, St. Francis de Asis and St. Patrick, as well as the Friars Preachers of the church of St. Dominic de Guzman, and the regular clergy of the Society of Jesus, of the church of St. Ignatius de Loyola and Santa Clara College. In the person of Rev. Father Alvarez, of the Franciscan College of Santa Barbara, as already

mentioned, the Order of the Friars Minor found a
worthy representative. For the rest, in the Eighth
Division, St. Joseph's Benevolent Society, marshaled
by Michael Kane, maintained its reputation as the
chief Catholic organization of San Francisco ; while,
in the Eleventh Division, composed of German citizens, shone brightly that loyalty to the ancient faith
which, despite Bismarck's blood-and-iron *régime*,
burns with pristine glow in the mighty Empire consecrated by the virtues of St. Boniface. The last
Division consisted of some sixty carriages, containing ladies and gentlemen. The picturesque and gallant bearing of the Independent MacMahon Guards,
recalled the "days of old" when the Irish Brigade
saved the honor of France at Fontenoy and on other
fields, as well as the achievements, in peace and in
war, of the most illustrious soldier of the age, the
President of the French Republic, himself a lineal
descendant of an ancient Irish house. The Guards
acted as an escort to the St. Mary's Total Abstinence
and Benevolent Society, the Laborers' Protective
Association, and the Knights of St. Patrick, a body
of prominent and patriotic Irish-Americans. And
here it should be said that to the energy, administrative ability and admirable arrangements of Mr.
James R. Kelly, Grand Marshal, and his efficient
colleagues, Hon. John Hamill and Hon. John M.
Burnett, Chief Aids, and Mr. P. J. Sullivan, Chief of
Staff, not a little of the *éclat* and success that attended the Centennial Celebration must in justice be
attributed. Let us cherish the hope that the labors

FATHER JUNIPERO SERRA.

of the humble followers of San Francisco de Asis—the
first Christian pioneers of Upper California—may ever
be held in honor, and that their memory, like the glory
of their **holy founder in** Heaven, may be perpetual.

The Apostle of Upper California.

THE venerable Padre Fray Junípero Serra, President
of the Franciscan Missionaries, and who **may,**
with truth, be styled **the** Apostle of Christian**ity to the**
gentile inhabitants **of Upper** California, **was born** in
the island of **Majorca, on the 24th of November,** 1713.
According **to the** "*Relacion Historica de la Vida,*"
written **by a Brother Religious, he** received in **baptism**
the name of Michael **Joseph, which, from his devotion**
to the companion of **the Seraphic Saint, he changed,**
on becoming **a member of the Order of** St. **Francis,**
for that of Junipero. It was **in the Convent** of St.
Bernardino, where his **elementary** studies were made,
that he formed the wish **of** devoting his life to the
immediate service of **God. At Palma, the capital of**
the island, he was, in his **sixteenth year, received as**
a member of the Order of St. **Francis, on the 14th of**
September, 1730. Some idea may **be** gleaned **of his**
aspirations, in early youth, of setting out **as a mis-**
sionary **to the** New World, from **his** remark **at a later**
period to **a friend·** "I had **no other** motive than **to**
revive in **my heart those glorious** designs **which I**
formed in my novitiate, **when** reading the lives of the

6*

Saints." From his religious profession, which took place on the 15th of September, 1731, he dated that improvement in his health which enabled him to perform the duties enjoined by the rule of his Order, when living in community, and subsequently to brave the perils and privations of an explorer of the savage wilds of America. While yet a student, he was appointed to a chair of Philosophy in the principal Franciscan college of his native island. So distinguished was his ability that, " before the end of the philosophical curriculum, he was honored by the University of the country with the honorary degree of Doctor of Divinity, and a chair of Theology." Disgusted with worldly honors, he determined to devote his life as a missionary priest to the conversion of the gentiles, and on the twenty-eighth of August, 1749, after recommending himself to God and our Blessed Lady, he embarked for America, in company with twenty other Religious. After many dangers by sea and land, Father Junípero, accompanied by only a single companion, arrived at theC ity of Mexico, on the 1st of January, 1750, having travelled from Vera Cruz— some fifteen hundred miles—on foot.

In June, 1750, in company with Father Francis Palou, Father Junípero, in obedience to the commands of his superiors, left the college of San Fernando, in Mexico, to take charge of a Mission in the territory of the Sierra Gorda, a vast, uncultivated region, inhabited by a gentile population to whom the Gospel had never been preached. In the Sierra Gorda the venerable missionary labored, with a zeal never surpassed, during a period of nine years. On his return to the Franciscan convent in the Mexican capital, Father Junípero was transferred to another field of effort. A Mission was established, under his government, at San Diego, the first in Upper California, and, for many years, the most important station on the northern coast. During the journey by land to San Diego a Mission dedicated to San Fernando, and the first formed by the Franciscan Fathers since their arrival in the country, was founded at Villacata, in Lower California. In mentioning the fact, Father Palou observes : "On the day following they commenced the foundations; the venerable Father-President being vested with alb and stole, blessed the holy water, and with it the site of the church, and the holy cross, which, being saluted as usual, was planted in front of the church. They named as patron, both for the church and Mission, the holy King of Castile and Leon, San Fernando. Having chaunted the first Mass, the President pronounced a most fervent discourse on the descent of the Holy Ghost and the establishment of the Mission. The sacrifice of the Mass being concluded, the " *Veni Creator* " was sung, the want of an organ and other musical instruments being supplied by the continual discharge of firearms during the ceremony, and the want of incense, of which they had none, by the smoke of the muskets."

On the feast of our Lady of Mount Carmel, July 16th, 1769, was founded at San Diego the first Mission in Upper California. So remarkable is the event that the annexed letter, dated July 3d, 1769, addressed

by the Father-President of the Franciscan Missionaries to his future biographer, Father Palou, will, without doubt, be read with deep interest :

"My Dear Friend:—Thank God I arrived the day before yes-
terday, the first of the month, at this port of San Diego, truly a
fine one, and not without reason called famous. Here I found
those who had set out before me, both by sea and land, except
those who have died. The brethren, Fathers Crespi, Biscaino,
Parron and Gomez, are here with myself, and all are quite well,
thank God. Here are also the two vessels, but the *San Carlos*
without sailors, all having died of the scurvy, except two. The
San Antonio, although she sailed a month and a half later,
arrived twenty days before the *San Carlos*, losing on the voyage
eight sailors. In consequence of this loss it has been resolved
that the *San Antonio* shall return to San Blas to fetch sailors for
herself and for the *San Carlos*.

"The causes of the delay of the *San Carlos* were: first, lack of
water, owing to the casks being bad, which, together with bad
water obtained on the coast, occasioned sickness among the crew;
and secondly, the error which all were in respecting the situation
of this port. They supposed it to be thirty-three or thirty-four
degrees north latitude, some saying one and some the other,
and strict orders were given to Captain Villa and the rest to keep
out in the open sea till they arrived at the thirty-fourth degree,
and then to make the shore in search of the port. As, however,
the port in reality lies in thirty-two degrees thirty-four minutes,
according to the observations that have been made, they went
much beyond it, thus making the voyage much longer than was
necessary. The people got daily worse from the cold and the
bad water, and they must all have perished if they had not
discovered the port about the time they did. For they were
quite unable to launch the boat to procure more water, or to do
anything whatever for their preservation. Father Fernando did
everything in his power to assist the sick; and although he
arrived much reduced in flesh, he did not become ill, and is now
well. We have not suffered hunger or other privations, neither
have the Indians who came with us; all arrived well and healthy.

"The tract through which we passed is generally very good land, with plenty of water; and there, as well as here, the country is neither rocky nor overrun with brushwood. There are, however, many hills, but they are composed of earth. The road has been in some places good, but the greater part bad. About half-way, the valleys and banks of rivulets began to be delightful. We found vines of a large size, and in some cases quite loaded with grapes; we also found an abundance of roses, which appeared to be like those of Castile. In fine, it is a good country, and very different *from old California.*

"We have seen Indians in immense numbers, and all those on this coast of the Pacific contrive to make a good subsistence on various seeds, and by fishing. The latter they carry on by means of rafts or canoes, made of tule (bullrush) with which they go a great way to sea. They are very civil. All the males, old and young, go naked; the women, however, and the female children, are decently covered from their breasts downward. We found on our journey, as well as in the place where we stopped, that they treated us with as much confidence and good-will as if they had known us all their lives. But when we offered them any of our victuals, they always refused them. All they cared for was cloth, and only for something of this sort would they exchange their fish or whatever else they had. During the whole march we found hares, rabbits, some deer, and a multitude of berendos (a kind of a wild goat).

"I pray God may preserve your health and life many years.

"From this port and intended Mission of San Diego, in North California, third July, 1769.   .

"FRANCIS JUNÍPERO SERRA."

That the "confidence and good-will" on the part of the gentiles, whereof the Father-President speaks with wonted charity in the foregoing letter, lacked stability, and could not be depended upon, is unhappily apparent from the fact that, during the absence of the expedition by land, commanded by Don Gaspar Portolá to discover and settle the port of Monterey, and which was composed of the commandant already mentioned, three officers, one sergeant, the Fathers Juan Crespí and Francisco Gomez, with twenty-six soldiers, seven muleteers, and fifteen Indians of Lower California—making in all a total of fifty-five Europeans and Indians—Father Junípero and his companions, two missionaries and eight soldiers, who remained at San Diego, were in great peril from the perfidious spirit of the gentiles. In order to obtain possession of the property belonging to the Religious, the savages attacked the newly-established Mission, in great force. "A perilous position, indeed," says the historian of "*The Catholic Church in California*," "it was, for the little band—ten or a dozen persons, without a fort, barricade or other means of defence save what a few hastily-erected huts could afford, and surrounded at the same time by hundreds of infuriated savages eagerly bent on their destruction, and armed with bows and arrows, spears, clubs and stones. The interposition of Heaven alone seemed capable of saving them in the emergency. On the 15th of the month, two days after the first attack had been made, the Indians in great numbers fell on the Mission and began plundering everything that came in their way. The soldiers were immediately put under arms, when the savages retired to a distance and began shooting their arrows. The firing was kept up with great vigor on both sides for a considerable time, till the enemy retired, having lost several in killed and wounded; the loss on the part of the Christians being only one killed and four wounded. **The result of** this engagement proved entirely different from what might **have** been expected. **Instead of either entirely** abandoning **the** place **and retiring to the mountains, or of reinforcing their numbers and making a** fresh attack on **the Christians, they returned with peaceful** dispositions, **begging the wounded to be cared for,** and **evincing, in their** manner, **a certain** salutary **fear and** respect, **which the recent defeat had created in** their **minds."**

Undismayed by the formidable difficulties that environed him, the venerable missionary pursued his apostolic labors with undiminished ardor. When the highest civil functionary at San Diego, finding that the supply of provisions was insufficient for more than a few weeks, and despairing of the safety of the vessel dispatched to the coast of New Spain for the necessaries of life—as the country was unable to afford the means of subsistence—informed the Fathers " that unless the vessel appeared by the 20th of March (the feast of St. Joseph, the patron of the Missions), he would embark the entire expedition, abandon the country, and return to Old California," the Father-President, we are informed, " determined to remain, and to trust to divine Providence for his support and protection ; but to retain the expedition was his principal concern. For this, one only means seemed capable of success—holy and fervent prayer, by which innumerable triumphs have been gained by the faithful in every age." It occurred to the Father that, through the intercession of St. Joseph, fervent petitions would find acceptance before the throne of God.

A Novena was begun, to be concluded on the 20th
of March, the day fixed for departure.   On the evening of the nineteenth—the last day of the exercises—
the long-expected *San Antonio* appeared.   In commemoration of the occurrence the venerable missionary, who had never ceased to put his trust in the
Almighty, and who recognized, with a heart overflow-
ing with gratitude, the special protection of Heaven,
resolved to celebrate annually a Mass to St. Joseph.
From San Diego, where he reclaimed from darkness
and the shadow of death one thousand and forty-six
souls, Father Junípero proceeded, in the *San Antonio*,
to Monterey, whereof he writes to Father Palou.   (The
first portion of the letter is given in pp. 12 and 13 of
the present work.   We give the concluding paragraph :)

" As it is a whole year since I received any letter from a Christian country, your Reverence may suppose in what want we are
of news ; but, for all that, I only ask you when you can get an
opportunity to inform me what the most Holy Father, the reigning Pope, is called, that I may put his name in the canon of the
Mass; also, to say if the canonization of the beatified Joseph
Cupertino and Serafino Asculi has taken place ; and if there is
any other beatified one, or Saint, in order that I may put them
in the calendar, and pray to them, we having, it would appear,
taken our leave of all printed calendars.   Tell me, also, if it is
true that the Indians have killed Father Joseph Saler, in Sonora,
and how it happened; and if there are any other friends deceased,
in order that I may commend them to God ; with anything else
that your Reverence may think fit to communicate to a few poor
hermits, separated from human society.   We proceed to-morrow
to celebrate the feast and make the procession of Corpus Christi,
(although in a very poor manner), in order to scare away whatever little devils there possibly may be in this land.

" Fr. Junípero Serra."

On the twenty-sixth of December, the first solemn baptism was performed by the Religious at the Mission of Monterey. We learn that, at the end of the third year from the date of their arrival, one hundred and seventy-five of the natives had been received into the Church.

In May, 1773, the followers of St. Dominic de Guzman having assumed charge of the Missions in Lower California, the sons of St. Francis, led by their Father-President, concentrated their force in Upper California, where " they quickly produced most remarkable results in the reduction of the country and the conversion of the natives." A Mission, under the invocation of St. Anthony of Padua, was established in the mountains of Santa Lucia, which yielded abundant fruit. Having changed the site of the Mission of San Carlos to a more favorable position, Father Junípero "transported there the neophytes and the cattle, and made it the headquarters for himself, never leaving it till the time of his death, except when engaged in establishing or visiting other establishments. At the same time, conformably to his orders, the Mission of San Gabriel was founded by Fathers Cambon and Somera, to the north of San Diego." Here the hostility of the Indians, under their chiefs, was appeased by the exhibition of a banner representing our Lady of Dolors. Before his departure from San Diego for Mexico, in October, 1772, the Father-President had founded the Missions of San Diego, San Carlos at Monterey, San Antonio, San Gabriel and San Luis Obispo. During his journey his life was in peril from a severe attack of malignant fever.   His requests having been granted by the Viceroy, Father Junípero left the Mexican capital in the autumn of 1773 for the scene of his labors, accompanied by several missionaries, officers and soldiers, and supplied with a large stock of provisions.   Compelled to put into the harbor of San Diego, Father Junípero proceeded by land, with a few companions, with the view of visiting the Missions.   An additional Mission, dedicated to San Juan Capistrano, was established between San Diego and San Gabriel—an event the joy of which was dimmed by the murder of Father Luis Jayme and the attempted destruction of the Mission.   When the sad intelligence reached the Religious at Monterey, the Father-President, we are told, exclaimed: " Thanks be to God, now the land has been watered, now the reduction of the people will be effected."   The presence of the Father-President upon the scene of conflict, as soon as he could leave Monterey, contributed in a great measure to the restoration of peace and the resumption of the work of conversion among the gentiles.   At the Missions of San Luis, San Gabriel and San Antonio, which he subsequently visited, the prospect, in a spiritual point of view, was most encouraging.   Of the Missions of San Francisco and Santa Clara some notice will be found elsewhere.

That the afflictions endured, with heroic fortitude, by this venerable servant of God were not wholly due to the ferocious savagery of the gentiles—the most degraded of mankind—is clear from the account which follows:

"On taking possession of the Missions of **Lower** California in 1668, Father Junípero **learned** that, in consideration **of the** difficulty **of** visiting the Missions, **his** Holiness Pope **Benedict** XIV. of illustrious memory, had conferred on the Fathers the privilege of administering the holy sacrament of Confirmation. As the same difficulty and necessity still existed, the Father-President, in order that the Christians might not be deprived of such a singular blessing, wrote to his superiors in Mexico, requesting them to apply to the Sovereign Pontiff for a like faculty for his brethren. The application was made and favorably received by the then reigning Pope, Clement XIV., who, for the reasons alleged, granted the same faculty for a period of ten years to the President of the Missions, and four others to be nominated by him. Immediately on receiving this power, Father Junípero lost no time in exercising it in behalf of his people. On the twenty-fifth of August, 1778, after administering the sacred rite to those prepared for it at his Mission of Monterey, he proceeded to the South, where he remained actively engaged till January of the following year, when he returned to San Carlos. Here he occupied himself in instructing and baptizing the neophytes, feeling happy that the work of the Missions was advancing as steadily and satisfactorily as could be reasonably expected; but this happiness, so natural in his case, was presently embittered, for at this time he was made acquainted of the appointment by the Supreme Council of Mexico of the Chevalier de la Croix as commandant and captain-general of the Californias. De la Croix was of all others the last man the Fathers would like to see appointed; he was entirely a different person from Bucarreli, for, although he affected to be in the interests of the missionaries, and desirous of promoting the cause of religion, he showed by his acts how unreal were his assertions. Amongst other impediments, which at the outset he threw in their way, may be mentioned that of preventing Father Junípero from exercising the faculty of confirming. On the plea that the Brief bestowing the privilege of confirming had not received the sanction of the government authorities, though in reality it had been submitted to and received the approval of the royal council of Madrid and the sanction of the authorities at Mexico, he prohibited the Father using it further till an order should be received to that effect from the Viceroy. No amount of reasoning or explanation could move him from his purpose, and so the Father had to submit to an order as capricious as unjust. The matter being finally referred to his Excellency, instructions were received not to interfere with the President of the Missions in the exercise of his duty, and even to grant him every facility for the discharge of his ministry.

During the time that the decision was pending, Father Junípero, in obedience to the order of the commandant, carefully abstained from exercising his right to confirm. He did not even make any visits to the other Missions, but occupied himself exclusively in instructing his flock at San Carlos. The decision was received in the month of September, 1781, when he resumed the exercise of his faculties, which should never have been suspended or even questioned, by the Governor. After confirming those prepared at the Missions of San Carlos and San Antonio, Father Junípero set out for the purpose of visiting the Missions of San Francisco and Santa Clara. This was not the first time he had been to these establishments, for, shortly after their foundation, he had paid them a visit. He was accompanied on the journey by his friend and disciple, Father Crespi, who was desirous of seeing the progress that religion was making in these parts. This was in the year 1781, and they arrived at the Bay on the twenty-sixth of October, where they remained till the ninth of November. During this time Father Junípero administered the Sacrament of Confirmation to all who had been converted since his previous visit, as also to those of the Mission of Santa Clara. The Father-President was now destined to undergo a loss which could not be readily repaired. While returning to San Carlos, a few days before arriving at home, his venerable friend and companion, Father Crespi, fell ill. We are not told what was the character of his sickness, but from the beginning it appears he had a presentiment of his speedy dissolution. Feeling that the hand of Death was upon him he prepared himself with much fervor for the reception of the last Sacraments, and with great confidence and love of God, resigned his soul into the hands of his **Creator**, on the first of January, 1782, being then in the sixty-first year of his age, and the thirtieth of his missionary career."*

The last years of the Father-President's eventful life, witnessed the founding of three Missions in the region immediately opposite the channel of Santa Barbara, between San Diego and Monterey, as well as the establishment of the pueblo of Los Angeles. After a visit to San Francisco, Father Junipero returned, in poor health, to Monterey, where he departed this life, in the odor of sanctity, on the 28th of August, 1784. In Upper California, eight Missions and five thousand eight hundred souls reclaimed from spiritual darkness, attested his apostolic labors. "He ended his laborious life," says Father Palou, "at the age of seventy years, nine months and four days, after having passed fifty-three years, eleven months and thirteen days in religion, and thirty-five years, four months and thirteen days, in the apostolic ministry, during which time he performed the glorious actions we have seen. He lived in continual activity, occupied in virtuous and holy exercises and wonderful exertions, all directed to the greater honor and glory of God, and the salvation of souls."

---

* "History of the Catholic Church in California," by W. Gleeson, M. A.

The Dominican Missions in Lower California.

IN May, 1773, the Religious of the Order of St. Dominic de Guzman assumed charge, by virtue of a rescript issued in the name of his Catholic Majesty, Charles III. of Spain and the Indies, of the Missions in Lower California founded by the regular clergy of the Society of Jesus, and subsequently served by Religious of the Order of St. Francis de Asis. The Missions entrusted to the Dominicans extended from San Diego to Cape San Lucas. Received with joy, respect and veneration by Cortez on their arrival in Mexico in June, 1526, the Friars Preachers had long illustrated, in the vast Aztec Empire subjugated by Spain, the devotion and fortitude which, at an earlier period, crushed the errors of the Albigenses in Languedoc and delivered Europe from an impious thraldom. In the Old World and the New, the victory had been won by the institution of the Rosary, the fruit of a special revelation from the Mother of God to St. Dominic. "Unless," said our Blessed Lady, "this celestial dew enriches the ungrateful soil, it will ever remain unfruitful." Among the first missionaries of the Order of Friars Preachers in Mexico were Fathers Thomas Ortez, Vincent of St. Mary, Thomas of Berlenga, Dominic of Soto and Just of St. Dominic—venerable servants of God, whose labors were worthy of Fathers Salva Tierra, Kühno and Junípero. Although, if we may judge from the terms of the Royal warrant from Madrid, the Franciscans were requested to make over to the Dominicans only a few of the Missions, Father Junípero and his brother Religious deemed it prudent, for the greater glory of God, to offer the whole of their spiritual charge in Lower California to the Friars Preachers. The proposition was accepted and ratified by the Viceroy in April, 1772. That the feeling of fraternal love which in the mediæval past animated the sons of St. Dominic and St. Francis, has not diminished, is apparent from the annexed circular addressed by the late Father Francisco Diego, Superior of the Franciscans on this coast, and subsequently the immediate predecessor, as first Bishop of Monterey, of his Grace the Most Rev. Archbishop Alemany :

" To the Reverend Fathers of San José, San Francisco de Asis, San Rafael, San Francisco Solano, Santa Cruz, San Juan Bautista and San Carlos of Monterey :

" VENERATED FATHERS AND BELOVED BROTHERS :—The Reverend Father-President of the Missions of Lower California Father Thomas Aumada, has made known to me that the Reverend Fathers thereof have enjoyed, during many years, a spiritual brotherhood with the Reverend Father Missionaries of Upper California, and that having succeeded to the charge of the Missions once occupied by the Fathers of the North, he desires and prays that the same brotherhood may still continue on the conditions which formerly existed. The mutual obligation agreed upon by the Missions of Upper and Lower California is to celebrate three Masses for each deceased Religious belonging thereto; and I, desiring that nothing be changed in this respect which may tend to consolidate and rivet the bonds of charity and union, and, at the same time, to give to the Dominican Fathers another proof of our affection, and to evince our gratitude for the many charitable offices performed in our behalf on our arrival at their Missions, pray that your Reverences may accept the brotherhood which the worthy Prelate has been so kind as to offer you.

"FR. FRANCISCO DIEGO.

" SANTA CLARA, June 12, 1838."

A similar agreement, we are informed, was made in 1854, between the Dominicans in California and the Franciscans of Santa Barbara.

In 1843, according to M. de Mofras, the following Missions in Lower California were under the direction of the Dominican Fathers of the Convent of Santiago in Mexico : San Miguel, Santa Catalina, Santo Tomas, San Vicente, Santo Domingo, Nuestra Señora del Rosario, San Fernando de Villecata, La Purisima (destroyed), San Luis (destroyed), Todos los Santos, Real de San Antonio (then the capital). San Francisco de Borja, Santa Gertrudis, San Ignacio, Santa Magdalena, Nuestra Señora de Guadalupe, Santa Rosalia de Molejé, San José Comandú, Nuestra Señora de Loreto (the former capital), San Francisco Xavier, San José del Cabo, and La Paz.   The Eduó, Pericué, Cochimie, Cora and Mouqui Indians, who at one time constituted the population of Lower California, no longer form distinct tribes, and are numerically insignificant.   When De Mofras visited the country, in 1843, the once flourishing Missions of San Miguel and Nuestra Señora de Guadalupe—the latter founded by Father Cavallero, President of the Dominican Missions—possessed only some three hundred Indians, and those of Real Loreto and Santo Tomas, a few hundred inhabitants respectively.   The other Missions, for the most part, were completely abandoned.   At San Francisco de Borja there were but six Indians; at San Ignacio, four families of the Spanish race; while at Jesus Maria there was not a single inhabitant.   Here and there, at other Missions, might be perceived a few small **farms cultivated** by white labor; and the preëminent **French observer notes** that the Mission of San **Vicente, in the** neighborhood of which was organized **a kind of** *pueblo*, **was the** only **one in Lower California which retained troops—a** company **of twenty soldiers stationed at that point** to repel the **incursions of the Yuma Indians, whose** stronghold was **on** the right bank **of the Rio** Colorado. **At** the Mission of San José del Cabo **died** the **ill**ustrious *savant*, Father Chappe **d'** Auteroche, who had **been sent by** the Royal **Academy of Sciences to observe the** transit **of Venus on the disk of** the sun, which **took place on the 3d of June, 1769. The** French **Acade**mician was **accompanied by two** distinguished officers of the Spanish **navy.** They determined, **with** precision, the position of Cape San **Lucas.**

As Lower California **possesses no rivers,** its aridity is extreme. **The climate is very hot and dry. The** territory contains **some good** harbors, and **abounds in** mineral wealth. The gold and silver mines of **Real** de San Antonio and the Mission of Santa Rosalia for**merly** attracted many laborers ; **and in** other parts of **the territory the** industrial **resources are** described **as** remarkable. While the **soil, it would** appear, **in the environs** of the **Missions of Rosario,** San Vicente, Nuestra Señora de Guadalupe, **San Miguel,** and Santo **Tomas is prolific** and susceptible **of cultivation, it** must, however, be allowed **that Lower California, re**claimed **from** barbarism by the **clergy of** the Society of Jesus, **presented, at the outset, from its** natural

7

disadvantages, greater obstacles to missionary enterprise than the territory subsequently reduced to civilization by the Franciscan Fathers.

To the Very Rev. Father Vilarrasa, Commissary
General and Superior of the Order of Preachers in
California, we are indebted for the subjoined extract
from the Acts of the General Chapter of the Dominican Order, held in Rome in 1777, which are kept in
the archives of the Master-General of the Order :

" We notify that the Catholic King of Spain, Charles
III., through his singular benignity towards our Order,
entrusted to our Religious of the Province of St. James
of Mexico the care of fourteen Missions in California,
and that twenty priests of the Order, with two lay-
brothers, were conveyed there from Spain at the Royal
expense, who, on their arrival, began to cultivate with
so much zeal the vineyard entrusted to them that soon
after, they, with God's assistance, led more than two
thousand idolaters to the Christian religion, and
founded two new Missions.   Wherefore, we earnestly
hope that all those barbarians shall be brought from
the miserable slavery of the Devil to the knowledge
and worship of the one and true God."

The cession of the Missions of Lower California to
the Dominicans is thus described in the *Exploration
du Territoire de l' Orégon, des Californies et de la Mer
Vermeille*, by De Mofras: " In the year 1771, the Marquis de la Croix's term of office as Viceroy having expired, was succeeded by the Baili de Bucarelli.   The
Dominicans of Mexico obtained a royal rescript (*une
cédule Royale du Roi d'Espagne*), by which the Francis-

cans were ordered to surrender to the Dominicans
the administration of one or two Missions. The Reverend Guardian of the College of St. Fernando re-
marked, with reason, that the province of Lower California (where most of the Missions were at that time),
could not be divided, that its limits were well defined, and that serious inconveniences would arise if
the two Orders were found in competition in the same
territory. He concluded by offering to the Dominicans, in case they would take exclusive charge of the
whole province (of Lower California) from Cape San
Lucas to the port of San Diego, to cede to them,
together with all the Missions then lately administered
by the Jesuits, also that of San Fernando de Villecata, and the five others which were yet to be established there. The Viceroy assembled the Council,
and on April 30, 1772, decreed that the above agreement should be carried into effect. It was not, however, until the 1st of May of the following year that
the Dominicans entered into definitive possession of
Lower California, and that the Franciscans retired
into Upper California; where, being able to concen-
trate (*concentrer*) all their efforts upon a territory less
extensive and more fertile, they soon obtained results which command admiration. At the end of
fourteen years, Father Junípero, who died in 1784,
had already founded fifteen Missions of Indians, or
villages of Spanish colonists."*

In California, the Order of St. Dominic is happily
flourishing. In 1850, the first church at Sacramento,

* De Mofras, volume 1, page 259.

under the invocation of St. Rose of Lima, was erected
by Rev. Father Peter Augustine Anderson, O. P., of
the Province of St. Joseph, U. S., who died in that
city from cholera. His remains were brought to Benicia
in 1854. At Martinez, Vallejo, Antioch, Pachecoville,
Somersville, Concord and Benicia, churches have been
built by the Friars Preachers; in San Francisco, two
tasteful structures, dedicated to St. Bridget and St.
Dominic, stand as monuments of their zeal and energy;
while, on the other hand, strange to say, the church
of St. Francis de Asis, in the same city, one of the
most elegant ecclesiastical edifices in the State, owes
its completion to the apostolic labors and noble charity
of the Dominican Fathers.

THE CHURCH IN CALIFORNIA

AS IT IS.

IN October, 1840, the Right Rev. Dr. Garcia Diego y Moreno, of the Order of St. Francis, was consecrated Bishop of Upper and Lower California. A native of Mexico, and some time Professor of Theology in a Franciscan convent in the land of his birth, Dr. Garcia Diego y Moreno was, at the period of his elevation to the episcopacy by Pope Gregory XVI., Commissary-prefect of the Missions of Upper California. On the death of the venerable prelate, which took place at Santa Barbara, April 30, 1846, the late Very Rev. Father Gonzales, Superior of the Franciscan Order in Upper California, became administrator of the diocese *ad interim*, the duties whereof he discharged until the appointment of the Most Rev. Joseph Sadoc Alemany, O. P., who was consecrated Bishop of Monterey, June 30, 1850, and translated to the Metropolitan See of San Francisco July 29, 1853. Born in 1814, at Vich, in Catalonia—a province of Spain, essentially Progresista in the real rather than the political meaning of the word—whose enterprising sons furnished the earliest Christian pioneers of South and Central America, Mexico and California, and whose literary fame has been illustrated by Balmes, the then Father Alemany was Provincial of his Order in the United States at the

time of his appointment by the Sovereign Pontiff to
the episcopal charge of Upper and Lower California.
Compelled, like the Irish ecclesiastical students of a
former age, to seek refuge on foreign shores from the
persecution of a bad government, the youthful candi-
date for the priesthood arrived in the Eternal City in
1836.   It was the unhappy era of so-called Liberalism
in the Iberian Peninsula when, under the auspices of
the British Minister at Madrid, Sir George Villiers,
subsequently known as Earl of Clarendon, Lord Lieutenant of Ireland, parasites and *protégés* of Lord Pal-
merston like Espartero and Mendizabal robbed the
Church and pursued the Religious Orders with a ma-
lignity which the Chancellor of the German Empire
seems to emulate in our own day.   Ordained priest at
Viterbo, in the Roman States, in 1837, where he held the
office of sub-master of novices, Father Alemany subsequently discharged the duties of an assistant priest in
the Dominican Church at Rome, popularly known as
the Minerva.   In 1840 Father Alemany arrived in the
United States, having, with another member of his
Order — the Rev. Father Francis Cubero — volun-
teered for the Mission in the State of Tennessee,
at the urgent request of the Right Rev. Dr. Miles,
of the Order of Preachers, Bishop of Nashville.   At
Memphis, where from his missionary labors in St.
Peter's Church, the name of the Archbishop of San
Francisco is still remembered with deep affection and
reverence, he resided for some years.   In 1848 he was
appointed Provincial of his Order in the United
States, having filled the position of President of the
Diocesan Seminary of Nashville with eminent distinc-

S ENGLAND ARCH.

Mary's College.

tion. In 1850 Father **Alemany left** for Rome **in** order to **be present at the** General Chapter **of the** Dominican **Order, and, on** his arrival **in** the capital **of** the Christian **world, was** consecrated Bishop **of Mon-** terey, and, **as we have had occasion to mention,** sub- sequently **translated to the diocese of San** Francisco, **which then** comprised **the** portions of California and Nevada lying between the Pacific Ocean and the **Colo-** rado River, and between 37° **7′ and** 42° North **lat.,** and which in 1860 extended north only **to the 39th** degree, **the** remainder **being erected into what is now the diocese** of Grass **Valley.**

The Very Rev. **Father** Vilarrasa arrived **in the** Uni- **ted** States from **Rome in** 1844, and remained until 1849, when he returned to the Eternal City, and, in **1850,** came **to California with Archbishop** Alemany.

Among the institutions **of the diocese, are the** fol- lowing:

St. Mary's **College, under the direction** of the Christian Brothers, **Rev. Brother Justin,** Visitor, President. **Number of** students, **over 250.**

Female Orphan **Asylum,** South **San** Francisco, con- **ducted by** the **Sisters of Charity.** Sister Francis McEnnis, Superioress, assisted **by** thirty **Sisters.** Orphans, four **hundred.**

Mount St. Joseph, Silver **Terrace, branch of the Female Orphan Asylum, Foundling and** Lying-in **Hos- pital conducted by twelve** Sisters **of Charity. Number of** children **and** infants, **two** hundred **and** fifteen.

Auxiliary **Orphan Asylum** in Hayes **Valley. Num-** ber **of Orphans,** thirty. Mission **school for boys; number of pupils,** one hundred **and fifty.**

Sacred Heart Presentation Convent, corner of Taylor and Ellis streets. Sister Mary Teresa Comerford, Superior, assisted by twenty-three professed Sisters, six novices and six postulants. Number of pupils attending school, eight hundred to nine hundred.

Presentation Convent and Free School, Powell street, Mother Mary Xavier Daly, Superior, assisted by twenty-six professed Sisters, five novices and six postulants. Children attending the school, seven hundred.

Hospital and Mercy House, conducted by the Sisters of Mercy, corner of Bryant and First streets, Mother Mary Joseph O'Rourke, Superior, assisted by twenty professed Sisters, six novices, and five postulants.

St. Joseph's School, conducted by the Sisters of Mercy. Number of pupils, three hundred and fifty.

St. Rose's School for girls, corner Fourth and Brannan streets, conducted by six Sisters of St. Dominic. Number of pupils, two hundred.

Convent of the Sisters of Notre Dame, at the Mission Dolores, select school for young ladies conducted by a branch of the Sisters of Notre Dame, of the Academy of San José. Number of pupils, four hundred.

Magdalen Asylum, on the old San Bruno road, conducted by eight Sisters of Mercy. Number of inmates, one hundred and five.

Free School for boys, attached to St. Mary's Cathedral, corner of California and Dupont streets; pupils, one hundred.

Free School, for boys, attached to the Church of St. Francis, Vallejo street. Number of pupils one hundred and fifty.

Free School, for boys, attached to St. Patrick's, Mission street. Pupils three hundred.

St. Joseph's School, for girls, conducted by the Sisters of the Holy Names of Jesus and Mary. Number of pupils, three hundred. School for boys attached to St. Joseph's, Tenth street. Pupils, four hundred.

St. Ignatius' College, Market street, conducted by the Fathers of the Society of Jesus. Very Rev. Aloysius Masnata, S. J., Superior; Rev. P. Bayma, S. J., President; Rev. J. Pinasco, S. J., Vice-President and Prefect of School, and many Professors. Number of pupils, six hundred.

Sacred Heart College, corner of Eddy and Larkin streets, conducted by the Christian Brothers, for day scholars. Number of pupils, seven hundred.

Male Orphan Asylum, San Rafael, Marin County, directed by Very Rev. James Croke. Orphans, about three hundred.

Dominican Convent, Benicia, Very Rev. Francis S. Vilarrasa, O. P., Superior, and eight Fathers, two students and four lay-brothers.

Novitiate of the Christian Brothers, Oakland. Number of Brothers, ten; novices, eight. A select school is conducted by the Brothers.

*7

Santa Clara College, directed by the Fathers of the Society of Jesus. Students, two hundred and fifty, besides forty others attending day school, taught by Professors of the College. The Rev. Father Brunengo, S. J., has recently succeeded the learned and esteemed Rev. Father Varsi, S. J., as President of the College.

St. Catherine's Convent and Female Academy, Benicia, under the care of the Sisters of St. Dominic. Twenty professed Sisters and six novices. Pupils, one hundred.

Convent and Academy of Notre Dame, Pueblo of San José, chartered by the State in 1868, conducted by the Sisters of Notre Dame. Sister Mary Cornelia, Superior, assisted by thirty Sisters. Boarders, two hundred; day-scholars, one hundred and fifty. Free scholars in separate schools, two hundred and fifty. Sunday-school girls, two hundred and eighty; boys, fifty.

Convent and Academy of the Most Holy Names, conducted by the Sisters of the Holy Names of Jesus and Mary, Oakland. Pupils, one hundred and fifteen.

St. Vincent's School, Mission and Third streets, San Francisco, conducted by the Sisters of Charity. Number of pupils, three hundred.

St. Vincent's School for girls, at Petaluma, Sonoma County, conducted by the Sisters of Charity. Sister Mary Catherine, Sister-Servant. Pupils, one hundred and fifty.

Free Schools, for girls, at Oakland, conducted by the same Sisters. Pupils, one hundred.

Santa Clara's Young Lady's Day School, by the Sisters of Notre Dame. Number of pupils, one hundred.

St. Patrick's College, Sacramento, conducted by the Christian Brothers. Number of pupils, one hundred.

Free School, for girls, at Sacramento, conducted by the Sisters of Mercy. Pupils, three hundred.

Free School, for girls, at Pueblo of San José, directed by the Sisters of Notre Dame. Pupils, one hundred and twenty-five.

Free School, for boys, at Sonora, Tuolumne County. Number of pupils, seventy-five.

Free School, at Stockton, San Joaquin County, attached to St. Mary's church. Pupils, one hundred and seventy-five.

Free and Pay Schools, for girls, at Vallejo, in charge of the Sisters of St. Dominic. Number of pupils, two hundred and fifty.

Free School, for girls, at Petaluma, directed by the Sisters of Charity. Pupils, sixty.

St. Gertrude's Academy, Rio Vista, conducted by the Sisters of Mercy.

In the Territory of Utah, temporarily placed by the Holy See under the administration of his Grace the Most Rev. Archbishop of San Francisco, there are, in addition to the Church of St. Mary Magdalen, at Salt Lake City, and two Chapels at Corinne and Ogden, served by two priests of the diocese, St. Mary's Academy, conducted by the Sisters of the Holy Cross, Mother Mary Augusta, Superioress, the number of pupils being one hundred and fifty, and the hospital in the Mormon capital, attended by the same Sisters.

While the Catholic population in the diocese of San Francisco amounts at present to some one hundred and twenty thousand, there are belonging to the same ninety-three churches, sixteen chapels, one hundred and twenty-one priests—fifty-one regular and seventy secular — twenty theological students, five Colleges, nine Academies, thirty-five select and parochial schools, four Asylums and five Hospitals.

When it is recollected that, in 1849, a small wooden shanty erected upon the site of the present tasteful Church of St. Francis, Vallejo street, was, with the exception of the church of the Mission Dolores, the only house of prayer in the commercial metropolis of the Pacific coast, the march of Catholic progress is evident. In June, 1851, a temporary chapel, under the invocation of the Apostle of Ireland—since replaced by the spacious structure on Mission street— was opened for public worship on Market street, the pastor Rev. Father Maginnis, who divided his services between St. Francis' church and St. Patrick's, being the only priest then in San Francisco who preached in the English language. After a time, followed the erection of the church and schools of St. Ignatius on Market street—at first small and insignificant, indeed, in dimensions—and subsequently, in close proximity to the original site, the present large and costly structures, rich with gilding, and suffused with the splendor and glowing with the bloom of

Italian art—that music, which, to adapt the thought of Lamartine, is **to** the eye what the strains of Rossini's *Stabat Mater* are **to the** ear—and the numerous religious edifices throughout the city which **are monuments of the piety and munificence of the** Catholic community.

As if to stimulate the faithful to **sustained** effort, **and to** dispel, by virtuous example, the clouds of anti-Catholic intolerance which for a time blackened all the horizon, the consecrated virgins of Catholic Sister**hoods** landed **upon our** shores. From **the quiet** shades **of St. Joseph's community, at Emmittsburg, in Maryland (the Mother-house of the Order in the United** States), **came** the daughters of St. Vincent de **Paul, on** their mission of love to the orphan; **and,** somewhat later, from the Island of **Saints, the Sisters** of Mercy—ministering angels and true children **of the** *Mater Misericordiæ*—to teach **the ignorant, to reclaim** from sin **and shame the** unfortunate Magdalen, **to** tend the sick and destitute, and **to** whisper solace and **hope to the dying. Nor should the** labors of the **Sisters of** St. Dominic, the **Sisters** of Notre Dame, **the Nuns of** the Presentation **Order,** and **the** other re**ligious** communities **of** females in the diocese and ecclesiastical Province of San Francisco, be forgotten in this brief notice of **Catholic progress in** California and Nevada.

THE PONTIFICAL FESTIVAL.

On **the second day of July, 1871, the** Catholic citi**zens of San Francisco, assisted by** delegations from the interior, celebrated with unbounded enthusiasm the twenty-fifth anniversary of the Pontificate of his Holiness, Pope Pius IX. Fifty thousand of the devoted children of the Holy Father participated in the manifestation of fidelity and filial love. The procession, numbering at least fourteen thousand persons by actual count, extended five miles in length, and was characterized by a leading organ of public opinion as the largest that '' has ever walked the streets of San Francisco, and, in proportion to population, has not been exceeded by any in the United States." In all the churches of the city, many of which were decorated with the Papal colors—white and yellow—High Mass was celebrated, and sermons were delivered indicating the grandeur of the occasion and the services rendered to civilization by the august dynasty of the Sovereign Pontiffs. The Grand Marshal and his Chief Aids were escorted by the Colonel and Staff of the Third Regiment of Infantry, and the First Division consisted of mounted squadrons of the National Guard, and barouches containing his Grace the Most Reverend Archbishop Alemany and the Right Reverend Bishop O'Connell, of Grass Valley, attended by members of the secular and regular clergy, and many prominent citizens. Among the conspicuous features of the procession were nineteen cars draped with alternate folds of white and yellow cloth, bearing twenty-five young ladies each, and '' symbolizing," as the Orator of the Day observed, '' the nineteen centuries of the Christian era." The universality of the Catholic Church was illustrated in the procession by delegations of the

French, Irish, Sclavonian, Chileno, English, Peruvian, Polish, Spanish, Californian, Brazilian, Kanaka, Austrian, Norwegian, **Greek,** Australian, **Panamaian, Mexican,** Chinese, **Italian, Russian, Scotch,** Guatemalean, **Prussian, Bavarian, Indian and African** nationalities. The programme of the Pavilion comprised the American "National Anthem," by all the Bands, the "Hymn of Pius IX.," Oration by Hon. Zach Montgomery, Reading of Dispatch to his Holiness, Grand *Te Deum*, and Benediction by the Most Reverend Archbishop. "The audience," it is stated in the account of the proceedings in the local press, "numbering probably not less than ten thousand people, devoutly knelt, while his Grace pronounced the words of blessing, in a clear and distinct voice." In the subjoined Resolutions adopted unanimously, and amid the hearty cheers of the immense audience, is apparent the loyal spirit that animates the Catholics of California ·

"The Catholics of **San Francisco, assembled** to celebrate the twenty-fifth **anniversary of our Holy** Father, **Pope Pius** IX., do resolve as follows :

" *First*—That **we hereby** tender **our** Holy Father, **in all** his **trials, sufferings and persecutions, our deep, sincere and** abiding **sympathy.**

" *Second*—That **to his** Holiness, as **the visible** head **of the true Holy Catholic and** Apostolic Church **of Christ our Lord, and to his successors in office, we** hereby pledge **our unswerving fidelity.**

" *Third*—That **we** regard **that small territory composed of the** Pontifical States **as the** rightful property of **the entire Catholic** world ; **sanctified by** the blood and tombs of her martyrs, enriched by our **treasures of art and learning,** and built up **and sustained by our contributions and the work of our hands.**

" Fourth—That we consider the late forcible invasion and seizure of the same by King Victor Emanuel as cruel and unjust, and that such deserves the reprobation of all candid and just men."

During the day a salute of twenty-five guns was fired, and at night the illumination was general throughout the city.

A SILVER JUBILEE.

Eloquent proof, if such were needed, of the triumph of the Catholic cause in California, may be found in the homage tendered to the venerable Metropolitan of the Province of San Francisco on the occurrence, in July, 1875, of the twenty-fifth anniversary of his Grace's episcopate. In the celebration of Archbishop Alemany's Silver Jubilee the clergy and the laity of the Golden State alike participated. While in all the churches of the diocese the holy sacrifice of the Mass was offered up for the spiritual and temporal welfare of the Archbishop, High Mass was celebrated at St. Mary's Cathedral by his Grace assisted by the Rev. Father Speckles as deacon; Rev. J. M. Cassin as sub-deacon; Rev. M. D. Slattery, first master of ceremonies; Rev. M. A. Bowman, second master of ceremonies, and Very Rev. J. Prendergast, Vicar-General. Right Rev. Bishop Amat, C. M., of Monterey and Los Angeles, Right Rev. Bishop O'Connell, of Grass Valley and Right Rev. Dr. Mora, Coadjutor Bishop of Monterey and Los Angeles, were present, as well as many of the secular and regular clergy of the Province. The attendance of the laity on the

occasion was **very** numerous. **At** one o'clock a
banquet was given in the basement **of the** Cathedral
by the clergy to **the** Archbishop, **who** presented his
Grace **with a set of vestments, valued at $1,500. The**
following **address was read on behalf of the** clergy,
and appropriately replied to by the Archbishop:

"MOST REV. ARCHBISHOP:—The clergy of the archdiocese have
thought this a fitting occasion on which to congratulate your
Grace on the special and great favor which Almighty God has
been pleased to show during the administration of the diocese
committed to your care, to allude, for the first time, to the successful accomplishment of the work assigned to you by God, in
this latest field of victorious Faith—to indorse your Grace's
course in the past and to pledge our support to your endeavors
in the future. In our reflections on the cradle-days of Faith,
that which strikes us as the most conspicuous and significant
feature of the latest creation of divine wisdom and love—the
Church—is the fact, that when our Blessed Lord launched the
bark of salvation, he placed at her helm a pilot (Peter) to
whom He committed her for the first quarter of the first of those
many centuries during which she was to cruise over a world
deluged with sin, bearing her precious burden of wrecked
humanity to a haven of lasting calm, security and happiness.
The occasion which brings us together to-day presents to us a
scene analogous to the rising of the Sun of Redemption in the
East some nineteen centuries ago—namely, the dawning of its
light in this latest and last field of Gospel triumph. And may
we not discern a parallel disposition of Divine Providence inau-
gurating the reign of revealed truth and heavenly morality in
this sunset of Christendom—as we may justly call it—namely,
the trust of the government of His Church to your Grace for a
like period of twenty-five years. This special favor attests the
approval of God, and argues well for the future career of the
Church in California.
" But the parallel does not end here—the formation and management of new dioceses by the sub-division of older ones—

which is the usual course adopted—present but few if any difficulties other than such as are connected with the government of
the old ones themselves; so that those who, by talent, learning
and experience, become familiar with the workings, and are
adjudged competent to hold part government of old dioceses,
may easily assume control of new ones, whose people, customs
and wants are similar to those in the fields they have just
vacated. Especially true is this when we consider the young
Bishop's access to the counsel of his old, experienced brother
prelates, should any emergency require it.

"Now, the work assigned by our Lord to his first Vicar, St.
Peter, was new and unlike to anything before it. Having
neither precedent to copy from, nor the experience of others to
assist him, he was left to his own resources, aided solely by God.
How like has been your mission ! Your Grace found yourself
on these remote shores in the midst of a heterogeneous people,
made up of portions of all the races on the globe, differing from each
other in national, political, social, religious, and moral traits; and
it was yours to harmonize those conflicting elements in so far as
religious unity demanded. The field of your labors was not old
Christendom, but a new domain, unsettled and unformed—a
field, *sui generis*, in which many of the rules of old countries,
worse than useless, had, in fact, to be discarded and new
rules framed as the new order of things demanded—a problem
truly puzzling where experience, in many respects, rather ham-
pered than helped. Old lessons in diocesan policy had often to be
unlearned, and new plans to be devised and adopted. Another
difficulty lay in the oft-changing and fast growing population
and their wants; so that all the provisions designed by your
Grace must needs be of such proportions as would meet the
requirements of a progressive and varying future. Still greater
courage, zeal and wisdom were demanded in your Grace's isola-
tion from brother prelates, whose advice might have been of
much service, had distance not precluded it; while the priests
for the most part have been young and strange, and have had to
rely on your counsel and guidance, rather than be able to assist
you by theirs, as old missionaries might have done. But, like

Peter, your **Grace** has bravely weathered the storm, skillfully piloted our bark clear **of the** shoals, and landed us safely in a goodly land, watered **by the dews** of heaven **and** abounding in the bread of **life.**

"Under your **Grace's** administration the Church has fairly distanced all her competitors in this new field of religious rivalry. With scarcely equal advantages, and without any earthly favor, the State in general, and this metropolis in particular, have become more and more Catholic with the advance of years. In a remarkably short period of time the chief wants of the Christian people have been amply provided for, and the many conveniences enjoyed by older communities have been placed within their reach. We would fain dwell on the many and varied institutions of the diocese; but time forbids more at present than a passing and summary allusion to them. So numerous are these monuments of your Grace's wisdom, charity and zeal, that the emblem of salvation surmounting them meets every eye. Hospitals supply a couch to the diseased and feeble. Asylums furnish a home to the orphan, **and a** refuge of **reform to the victims of vice.** Schools unfold **their treasures of Christian wisdom and** love. **Convents afford to sensitive and fervent souls a sanctuary** from **the blighting blasts of worldiness.** **Churches** everywhere open wide their doors to the suppliant; spacious sanctuaries are spread with the banquet of divine love. **Altars have been erected wherever the prophecy** of Malachi has **at length been** literally **and completely fulfilled,** for ' **in every place there is a sacrifice, and there is offered to my name a clean oblation . . . even to the going down of the sun.'**

"**What more could you, or those who are most devoted to your Grace, wish for, if it be** not the continuance of the triumphs **already achieved?** The sub-division of the vast sphere of your **labors into** other dioceses, gives to those **triumphs a character of permanence which assures** their existence **throughout time with the** universal and indefectible Church **of Christ.**

"We **regard the success of your Grace's career and the consequent blessings we, your spiritual** children, **enjoy, as due, under God, to the assiduous cultivation and practice of Apostolic zeal,**

such as infuses into man's efforts far more continuous and untiring energy than any earthly interests could inspire—evidence
that the sacrifices made under its influence are prompted by
higher than material or ephemeral considerations of prudence—
so necessary to moderate that zeal and to restrain the soul fired
by it from blind and impetuous attempts to attain ends without
the possession and use of proportionate means; of charity
unbounded, making one all to all and suffering no distinction of
persons, so indispensable to the leadership of the cosmopolitan
association of humanity of which this community is composed;
of simplicity, personal disinterestedness, self-privation and
poverty, and other kindred virtues, with which God has been
pleased to adorn the chief pastor of this diocese.

"We have as yet said nothing of the feeble part which God
has permitted ourselves to take in the grand work performed by
your Grace; but modesty should not, on an occasion like this,
prevent us from at least avowing our sincere and cherished
attachment to your Grace—our readiness, ever and always, to
spend our best efforts, and, if needs were, to lay down our lives
to secure the successful result of your Grace's undertakings.
However conscious we may be of our own faults —and we know
them well—we can appreciate noble deeds in a noble cause; and
therefore we would fain take this opportunity of stamping our
hearty endorsement on your Grace's labors, while we beg your
indulgent forgiveness of our delinquencies in the past. For we
are convinced that we have not been as deserving of your
approval as you have been of our commendation, veneration,
esteem and love.

"Lastly, we would renew and repeat to-day the pledge given
on our affiliation to the diocese, of our fealty to the sacred office,
and our profession of undying devotion to the person of your
Grace. We want no exchange for the guide whom God has
graciously given to us. All we ask for are the virtues and graces
required to make us faithful, willing and ready supporters of
your Grace's endeavors for the welfare of the diocese in the
future. And as some compensation to you for our many short-
comings, we will pray, as we have prayed to-day, that our Divine

Lord, who has already given to your Grace the years of His first Vicar, Peter, may continue them through the years of His latest Vicar, Pius, and then on, till the measure of your Grace's merits can hold no more.

"We beg, in conclusion, that your Grace will be pleased to accept the small offering which we present on this joyful day—not as a measure or guage, but as a token of the esteem and veneration of the priests of the diocese of San Francisco for their spiritual Father and chief."

At three o'clock, many prominent Catholic citizens of San Francisco assembled in the parlors of the Archbishop's residence. When the applause that greeted his Grace's entrance subsided, Mr. A. H. Loughborough read the annexed address of the laity of San Francisco:

" MOST REVEREND AND BELOVED FATHER :—With joyful hearts your children celebrate the twenty-fifth anniversary of your episcopate, and we come to offer you the cordial congratulations, and assure you of their sincere gratitude and devoted love.

" With self-sacrificing zeal for religion you consented to leave the congenial quiet of your convent life, and, taking with you the humble habit and severe discipline of your Order, assume the arduous labors and responsible cares of the Episcopal See. The work of a pioneer bishop is ever Apostolic, but the history of no country affords a precedent for the peculiar obstacles to the culture of religion that were found in California during the early days of American occupation, and which to a great extent still continue to exist. Many of the difficulties that stood in the way of your great mission were apparent to all; but no doubt there were many more that have been buried in your patient silence.

"Thanks to your assiduous and persevering toil for five and twenty years, the flock under your pastoral care enjoy to-day all the benefits of Catholic civilization. We have churches convenient to almost every family, attended by zealous and efficient pastors, and filled with large and devout congregations; we have numerous schools and colleges, and hospitals and asylums, all conducted by the appropriate religious Orders of men and women consecrated to works of charity and the education of youth—in a word the prosperity of the Church has kept pace with the rapid growth of this young and vigorous State.

"We do not forget, however, that the period which appears short for the accomplishment of so much work, has brought the devoted laborer to the threshold of old age, and that, while the growth of the flock demands of this venerable pastor longer and more frequent journeys, and imposes on him new and more constant burdens, his wonted strength, if not nursed with more tender care, must soon begin to fail. In the hope, then, that you will, for the sake of your flock, use that precious strength more sparingly hereafter, and indulge it with at least some of the little comforts which it needs, but which your self-denial has heretofore rejected, we beg that you may be pleased to acccept the small donations contributed by a few friends, and offered on this happy occasion, with fervent prayers that Heaven may long preserve the life of our dear Archbishop."

Mr. Loughborough then presented his Grace with a check for $5,000, the gift of the laity of San Francisco. The Archbishop, with emotion which was shared by all present, replied as follows :

"Well, really, I have no words with which to answer these— I will not call them heresies, because there is no heresy except in the extravagant language employed; but I certainly ought to question the correctness and accuracy of the statements made. This is not my work. Of course, I could not resist the command of the Holy Father when he required and ordered me to come out here as an Apostolic Bishop. God, in His infinite goodness, has been pleased to grant the increase. I certainly think that all this talk is rather a compliment that is due to you and the general clergy of the Province of California. The constant, never failing, generous offerings and noble gifts of this Province, and particularly of this diocese, coupled with the generous spirit of co-operation, it is well known, has elevated the Church into what it is. The noble co-operation of the clergy, under the providence of God, from the time that I had the pleasure of visiting Dublin, seems to have followed me here. It appears that some guardian angel sent me there, and from that time I have never failed to obtain a large accession of clergy, whose zeal has devoted their lives to the service of God upon these distant shores, in order to establish the Church and to sustain the interests of Religion. I therefore take occasion on this celebration day, to thank heartily and sincerely all the Catholics of the diocese, and of the Province, and all the clergy, for their hearty co-operation, and their candid feeling and wishes, and for these rich offerings. I hope Almighty God will bless you for the bountiful, noble and Apostolic success which the Church has met with on this coast."

Miss Agnes Tobin, a daughter of Mr. Richard Tobin, accompanied by Miss Bella Sullivan, read a filial address to his Grace, and presented a purse of money with a silver basket, which the Archbishop gratefully acknowledged, expressing at the same time the hope that the "rising Catholic young ladies would furnish abundant material for the work of Religion in the ranks of the holy women, who have left the world to follow Christ." After the announcement by the Very Rev. Father Prendergast, Vicar-General, that a carriage and pair of horses, the gift of Colonel Peter Donahue, were at the Archbishop's disposal, addresses were delivered by Miss Gates, of the Sacred Heart Convent, at Oakland, and Miss Lavinia O'Neill, on behalf of our Lady of Mercy's School, Rincon Hill, for which his Grace briefly returned thanks. The former young lady presented a model of a gondola worked

in white satin embroidered in silver, and a silver dish
and pitcher, and the latter, a silver basket and a
purse containing $50.

In the evening, after service in St. Mary's Cathedral, the members of the Catholic societies tendered
their respectful homage and congratulations to the
Archbishop.   The subjoined address and resolutions, which were beautifully printed and illuminated
in gold and colors and bound in red morocco by
P. J. Thomas, were presented on behalf of St.
Joseph's Benevolent Society:

"MOST REV. DEAR ARCHBISHOP: The occurrence of the twenty-
fifth anniversary of your translation to this Archdiocese is an
occasion of congratulation to your faithful children. While, in
common with others, we deem it our pleasure to lay before you
our duty and affection, we thank Almighty God for having spared
you to us. Your administration, fraught with all the trials and
anxieties of building up the Church in a new country, has been
so successful, that it must be a cause of extreme joy to you, as
our supreme pastor, to receive the united manifestations of
approval by your flock.

"We are but a fraction of the many institutions of charity and
benevolence fostered and cherished by your paternal care. We
have prospered; our membership has increased year by year,
and the good we have done in the spirit of Christian charity and
love receives its tone from your kind and watchful solicitude.
May you live many years to sustain and see fulfilled to an ample
fruition all the beautiful institutions which you have assisted to
establish. May you also continue to receive our affection and
love. And when the term of this life, which is so surely marked
out for us all, has drawn to a close, may you bear to the happy
destiny that awaits you our prayers and our gratitude.

"At a meeting of the Council of our Society, held July 20th,
the following resolutions were unanimously adopted:

" WHEREAS, his Grace the Most Rev. Archbishop Alemany has presided over our spiritual welfare generally for twenty-five years, and especially as a society for fifteen years: AND WHEREAS, during all that time we have recognized him as a fitting and legitimate delegate of Apostolic authority and a living exemplar of the truths he taught: AND WHEREAS, amid all the vicissitudes of our society he has ever shown himself a true friend and father, conferring innumerable favors, counseling, exhorting, advising: AND WHEREAS, he has always been to us a tender and watchful shepherd, never withholding a helping hand in moments of doubt and danger: THEREFORE, be it

Resolved, That we tender to him our heartfelt devotion as Catholic subjects, and our gratitude and love as members of St. Joseph's Benevolent Society: AND FURTHERMORE, be it

Resolved, That in view of his long career of piety and usefulness among us, from the early days when the flock was scattered and the labor arduous down to the present time, when the fold is denser though the care is not less severe, we rejoice in having an opportunity to congratulate him on the completion of twenty five-years of heroic exertion and success, and the possession of the love of a zealous and devoted people; and to also express our hope that his days may be far prolonged to continue the glorious work of his episcopal ministrations."

Mr. James R. Kelly, on behalf of the Society, then presented his Grace with a ciborium of California silver.

The President of St. Paul's Benevolent Association of St. Boniface's church delivered on the occasion an address to the Archbishop in the German language, thoroughly eulogistic of his Grace's career.

8

MONTEREY AND LOS ANGELES.

The present Bishop of Monterey and Los Angeles, the Right Rev. Dr. Amat, of the Congregation of the Mission, was consecrated March 12, 1854. The consecration of the Right Rev. Dr. Mora as Bishop of Mossynopolis, *in partibus infidelium*, and Coadjutor of Bishop Amat, took place August 3, 1873. Like the Most Rev. Archbishop of San Francisco, both prelates are natives of Catalonia in Spain.

The literary and religious institutions of the diocese, which comprises that portion of California that lies South of 37° 13′ North latitude, and extends eastward to the Colorado River, are : St. Vincent's College, Los Angeles, under the Rev. Fathers of the Congregation of the Mission of St. Vincent de Paul. Very Rev. M. Flynn, C. M., Superior. Number of boarders, fifty.

Franciscan College of Santa Barbara, conducted by the Rev. Fathers of the Minor Order of St. Francis of Assisium ; Rev. Joseph Maria Romo, Guardian. Number of boarders, seventy.

College of Our Lady of Guadalupe, at Santa Inez, conducted by the Franciscan Brothers. Brother Bernard, Director. Number of boarders, fifty.

Charitable Institution of Los Angeles, directed by the Daughters of Charity. Sister Scholastica Logedon, Sister-servant. Three hundred pupils, one hundred boarders.

County Hospital of Los Angeles, conducted by the Daughters of Charity.

St. Vincent's Institution of Santa Barbara, conducted by the Daughters of Charity. Sister Polycarp O'Driscol, Sister-servant. Average number of pupils, one hundred and fifty; boarders, seventy.

Academy of the Holy Cross, at Santa Cruz, directed by the Daughters of Charity. Sister Rosanna Smith, Sister-servant. One hundred and fifty pupils; boarders, forty.

Male Orphan Asylum, at Pajaro Valley, near Watsonville, attached to the Church of the Immaculate Heart of Mary. Number of orphans, forty.

Convent, Asylum and Academy, at San Juan Bautista, conducted by the Sisters of the Most Holy and Immaculate Heart of Mary. Five hundred pupils; boarders, twenty. Sister Carmen Argelaga, Superior. This house is the novitiate of the same order.

Convent and Academy of Mary Immaculate, for young ladies, at Gilroy, Santa Clara County, directed by the Sisters of the Most Holy and Immaculate Heart of Mary. Sister Mencia Martorano, Superior. Pupils, fifty.

Academy of the Immaculate Heart of Mary, for young ladies, at San Luis Obispo, conducted by the Sisters of the Most Holy and Immaculate Heart of Mary. Sister Raymunda Cremadell, Superior; number of pupils, seventy.

The Catholic population of the diocese is about 34,000, and the Catholic Indian population, some 3,000; the Indian settlements Santa Isabel, Pala,

Pauma and Temascal being regularly attended. There are thirty churches, three churches in ruins, eleven chapels, thirty-two stations, thirty-two secular priests in parishes, nine priests belonging to Religious Orders and six ecclesiastical students in colleges in Europe.

GRASS VALLEY.

The diocese of Grass Valley, erected by a Bull of his Holiness Pope Pius IX., on the 22d of March, 1868, comprises the part of California from 39° to 42° North latitude, and extends from the Pacific Ocean to the eastern boundary of the State of Nevada. The Right Rev. Dr. O'Connell, a native of Ireland, formerly one of the directors of the Foreign Missionary College of All-Hallows, Drumcondra, at Dublin, in Ireland, and some time a missionary in the diocese of San Francisco, was consecrated February 3, 1861, Bishop of Flaviopolis, *in partibus infidelium*, and Vicar Apostolic of Marysville, and translated to Grass Valley, March 22, 1868. The Catholic population numbers some 14,000. There are twenty-five priests, thirty-five churches, five clerical students in All-Hallows College in Ireland, one clerical student in the Sulpician Seminary at Baltimore, in Maryland, seventy stations, and the subjoined religious, literary and charitable institutions :

Missionary Seminary of the Congregation of the Precious Blood of Christ, Rohnerville, Humboldt county. The object of this institution is to supply a sufficient number of priests for giving missions and retreats. Five priests, five ecclesiastical students, and three lay Brothers form the present community. Very Rev. Joseph Uphaus, Superior.

St. Joseph's College, Rohnerville, Humboldt county. Under the direction of the priests of the Most Precious Blood, Rev. Joseph Alphons, C. PP. S., Superior.

Convent of the Sisters of Mercy, at Grass Valley ; number of Sisters, fourteen ; Rev. Mother Mary Baptist, Superior.

Convent of the Sisters of Charity, at Virginia City, Nevada. Number of Sisters, eleven ; Sister Vibiana, Superior.

School for girls and small boys, conducted by the Sisters of Mercy, at Grass Valley. Number of scholars, two hundred.

St. Mary's School, Virginia City, Nevada, conducted by the Sisters of Charity. Number of scholars, three hundred and sixty-eight.

St. Joseph's Convent of Mercy, Eureka, Humboldt county, established June, 1871.

St. Joseph's Convent of Mercy, Yreka, Siskiyou county, established February, 1871.

St. Patrick's Parochial School, Gold Hill, Nevada.

Holy Angels' Female Orphan Asylum, under the care of the Sisters of Mercy. Number of orphans, sixty. There are in charge six professed Sisters and five novices.

St. Patrick's Male Orphan Asylum, under the care of the Sisters of Mercy. Number of orphans, forty. There are three professed Sisters in charge.

Nevada Orphan Asylum, in Virginia City, Nevada, under the charge of the Sisters of Charity. Number of full orphans, one hundred ; half-orphans, sixty-eight.

St. Mary's Day School, under the care of the Sisters of Charity. Number of day-scholars, two hundred. The community consists of eleven Sisters ; five young ladies assist as teachers. The buildings are so located that the orphans and day-pupils are graded together in class. The Sisters visit and help the sick poor. Number of sick visited, five hundred.

———————

From the time when, in 1840, the Right Rev. Dr. Garcia Diego y Moreno, of the Order of St. Francis, was Bishop of Upper and Lower California—suffragan to the Metropolitan See of Mexico (in the administration of which that revered prelate was succeeded in 1846 by the Very Rev. Father Gonzalez, of the same Order, as Vicar-Capitular)—how marvelous has been the development of Catholic interests on the Pacific slope ! Truly, in the words of Mr. Loughborough, "the prosperity of the Church has kept pace with the rapid growth of this young and vigorous State." "A hundred years ago" exclaims, in eloquent language, Hon. J. W. Dwinelle, "how feeble was the Catholic Church in the United States. To-day how strong she is—strongest among the strong. A hundred years ago proscribed, her name a reproach !

to-day, proud in the consciousness of her strength, her children are free to ask for every thing—to receive it. They can be legislators, Governors, Senators and Judges; one of them was Chief Justice of the United States for twenty-five years. And the example of the forty million citizens of the United States has not been lost upon other peoples. Is it not true that where the English language is now spoken, the Catholic Church is practically free? That, although there may be enactments against her on the statute books, they are in effect dead, and cannot be enforced? Where is she stronger at this day than in the United States? Where are her foundations broader, deeper, more solid? Where are her hospitals, her convents, her colleges, her churches in a more flourishing condition? And does this not demonstrate that her material strength lies in the law of voluntary contribution, and in those free political institutions which ' *let her alone?* ' "

And, in view of the triumph of the Faith in the Eastern States, as well as in England, India and throughout the British Empire, the victory of the Catholic cause in California, despite intolerance and persecution in Mexico and South America, is a significant sign of the times, full of consolation and joy.

The Pious Fund of California.

APPENDED is a brief history of the Pious Fund (*Fondo Piadoso de California*), prepared by John T. Doyle, Esq., of the San Francisco bar, acting as the attorney-in-fact of his Grace the Most Reverend Archbishop Alemany and of the suffragan Bishops of the Province, against the Republic of Mexico, on behalf of the Catholic Church of the State of California, and all others beneficially interested in the Pious Fund of California. The Most Reverend and Right Reverend claimants demonstrate, in a Memorial, that " the Republic of Mexico is liable to the Catholic Church of California in a large sum of money, exceeding, according to the best information they can obtain, $1,700,000 in gold coin of the United States, for the portion belonging to said Church of California, of the interest which has accrued since the 2d of February, 1848, on the capital of the Pious Fund of the Californias, which was incorporated into the National Treasury of the Republic of Mexico, by and in pursuance of the decree of the Provisional President of said Republic, dated October 24th, 1842, and on which capital the said Republic of Mexico, by the same decree, undertook and promised to pay interest, at the rate of six per centum per annum, thenceforth." Mr. Doyle, in his lucid and admirably written historic *résumé*, observes :

" From the time of the discovery of California in 1534 by the expedition fitted out by Cortez, the colonization of that country and the conversion of its inhabitants to the Catholic faith was a cherished object with the Spanish Monarchs. Many expeditions for the purpose were set on foot, at the expense of the Crown, during the century and a half succeeding the discovery, but though attended with enormous expense, none of them were productive of the slightest good result. Down to the year 1697 the Spanish Monarchs had failed to acquire any permanent foothold in the vast territory which they claimed under the name of California.

"The success of the Jesuit Fathers in their Missions on the northwestern frontier of Mexico, and elsewhere, induced the Spanish Government as early as 1643 (on the occasion of fitting out an expedition for California under Admiral Pedro Portal de Casanata,) to invite that Religious Order to take charge of the spiritual ministration of it and the country for which it was destined, and they accepted the charge; but that expedition, like all its predecessors, failed.

"The last expedition undertaken by the Crown was equipped in pursuance of a royal cédula of December 29, 1679. It was confided to the command of Admiral Isidro Otondo, and the spiritual administration of the country was again entrusted to the Jesuits, the celebrated Father Kino [Kühno] being appointed Cosmógrafo Mayor of the expedition. Various circumstances conspired to delay its departure, and it only sailed on the 18th of March, 1683. Many precautions had been taken to ensure its success, but after three years of ineffectual effort and an expenditure of over $225,000 it was also abandoned as a failure; and at a junta general, assembled in the City of Mexico under the auspices of the Viceroy, wherein the whole subject was carefully reviewed, it was determined that 'the reduction of California by the means theretofore relied on was a simple impossibility,' and that the only mode of accomplishing it was to invite the Jesuits to undertake its whole charge, at the expense of the Crown. This proposition was made; but it would seem that the conduct of the royal officers, civil and military, must have contributed to the previous failures, and probably for that reason it was declined by the Society, although the services of its members as missionaries were always freely placed at the disposal of the Government.

"Individual members of the Society, however, animated by a zeal for the spread of the Christian faith in California, proposed to undertake the whole charge of the conversion of the country and its reduction to Christianity and civilization, and this without expense to the Crown, on condition that they might themselves select the civil and military officers to be employed. This plan was finally agreed to, and on the 5th of February, 1697, the necessary authority was conferred on Fathers Juan Maria Salva Tierra and Francisco Eusebio Kino, [Kühno] to undertake the reduction of California, on the express conditions, however: 1st. That possession of the country was to be taken in the name of the Spanish Crown; and 2d. That the royal treasury was not to be called on for any of the expenses of the enterprise, without the express order of the King.

"In anticipation of this result, Fathers Kino [Kühno] and Salva Tierra had already solicited and received from various individuals and religious bodies, voluntary donations called *limosnas*, or alms, contributed in aid of the enterprise. The funds thus collected were placed in their hands, in trust, to be applied to the propagation of the Catholic faith in California by preaching, the administration of the sacraments of the church, erection of church edifices, the founding of religious schools and the like—in a word, by the institution of Catholic Missions there under the system so successfully pursued by the Jesuits in Paraguay, Northern Mexico, Canada, India, and elsewhere.

"The earliest contributions thus obtained will be found detailed in Venegas' '*Noticias de la California*,' vol. 2, p. 12. Besides sums given to defray immediate expenses, it was determined to establish a fund, or capital, the income from which should form a permanent endowment for the Missionary Church. Towards this latter object the first recorded contributions seem to have been by the congregation of N. S. de los Dolores, which contributed $10,000, and Don Juan Caballero y Ozio, who gave $20,000 more. These donations formed the nucleus of the fund destined for the propagation of the Catholic faith in California. It was increased from time to time by others, and in a comparatively few years attained magnitude and importance. It was invested and administered by the Jesuits in pursuance of the trust on which it was confided to them, and its income was the source from which was defrayed the annual expense attending the Missions in California. In time it acquired by common acceptance the name of ' The Pious Fund of the Californias.'

"Among the most important contributions to the fund was one by the Marquis de Villa Fuente and his wife, who, in 1735, in addition to large previous donations, conveyed to the Society of Jesus, by deed of gift, *inter vivos*, estates and property of great value and productiveness.

"During the seventy years that the Jesuits pursued the spiritual conquest of California, they gradually extended their Missions from Cape San Lucas up the peninsula, to the northward; and at the period of their expulsion they had established those of San José del Cabo, Santiago de las Coras, Todos Santos, Francisco Xavier, Nuestra Señora de Loreto, San José Comandú, La Purísima de Cadegomo, Nuestra Señora de Guadalupe, Santa Rosalia de Molejé, San Ignacio, Santa Gertrudes, San Francisco de Borja, Santa Maria de Los Angeles, and these, with that of San Fernando de Villacata, founded by the Franciscans in May, 1769, were all the Missions of Lower California.

"At this time the interior of Upper California was unexplored, and its eastern and northern boundaries uncertain. The outline of the coast had been mapped with more or less accuracy by naval exploring expeditions fitted out by the Crown, and by the commanders or pilots of the Phillipine galleons, which, on their return voyages to Acapulco, took a wide sweep to the north, and sighted the leading headlands from as far north as the 'Cabo-blanco de San Sebastian,' down to Cape San Lucas. The whole coast, as far north as Spain claimed, was called by the name of California. The terms Upper and Lower California, only came into use after the division and distribution of the Missions between the Dominicans and Franciscans, hereafter noted.

"The Pious Fund continued to be managed by the Jesuits, and its income applied in conformity to the will of its founders, and the Missions of California remained under their charge down to

1768, in which year they were expelled from Mexico in pursuance of the order of the Crown, or pragmatic sanction of February 27, 1767. Their missions in California were directed by the Viceroy to be placed in the charge of the Franciscan Order. Subsequently a royal *cédula* of April 8, 1770, was issued, directing that one-half of these Missions should be confided to the Dominican Friars; in pursuance of which, and a ' *concordato* ' of April 7, 1772, between the authorities of the two Orders, sanctioned by the Viceroy, the Missions of Lower California, and the whole spiritual charge of that peninsula, were confided to the Dominicans and those of Upper California to the Franciscans. The income and product of the Pious Fund was thereafter appropriated to the Missions of both Orders.

" The Church when first established in Upper California, was purely missionary in its character. Its foundation dates from the year 1739; in July of which year Father Junípero Serra, a Franciscan friar, and his companions, reached the port of San Diego, overland, from the frontier Mission of Lower California, and there founded the first Christian Mission and first settlement of civilized men, within the territory now comprised in the State of California. Their object was to convert to Christianity and civilize the wretched native inhabitants, sunk in the lowest depths of ignorance and barbarism. In pursuit of this object, they exposed themselves to all the perils and privations of a journey of forty-five days across an unexplored wilderness, and a residence remote from all the conveniences and necessaries of civilized life, in the midst of a hostile and barbarous population who requited the charity of the Christian missionary with the crown of Christian martyrdom. Father Junípero and his followers established Missions among these barbarous people, from San Diego as far north as Sonoma, at each of which the neighboring tribes of Indians were assembled and instructed in the truths of the Christian religion and the rudiments of the arts of civilized life. The Missions of Upper California, and the dates of their foundation, were as follows:

" San Diego, 1769; El Carmelo, 1770; San Fernando, 1771; San Gabriel, 1771; San Antonio, 1771; San Luis Obispo, 1772; San

Francisco de Asis, 1776; San Juan Capistrano, 1776; **Santa Clara**,
1777; San Buenaventura, 1782; Santa Barbara, 1786; La Purísima, 1787; Santa **Cruz**, 1791; La Soledad, 1791; San Miguel,
1797; **San Juan** Bautista, 1797; **San José**, 1797; San Luis Rey,
1798; **Santa Ynes**, 1802; **San Rafael**, 1817; **San** Francisco Solano,
1823.

"**The Missions were designed,** when the population should be
sufficiently instructed, to be converted into parish churches, and
maintained as such, as had already been done **in** other parts of
the viceroyalty **of New Spain;** but in the meantime, and while
their missionary character continued, they were under the eccle-
siastical government of a President of the Missions. Father
Serra was the first who occupied this **office,** and **the Missions
were governed and directed by him and** his successors as such,
down to the year 1836, when this officer was superseded in his
**authority by the appointment of a bishop and the erection of
the** Californias **into an episcopate or diocese.**

"Francisco Garcia Diego, the last President of these Missions,
was also the first bishop of **the new diocese.**

"**The text of the decree or pragmatic sanction expelling the
Jesuits from the Spanish dominions, is very brief. The only provision on the subject of property** contained in it **is in the words:**
'*y que se ocupen todas las temporalidades de la compañia en mis
dominios.*' **Under this provision, the Crown took all the** estates
of the Order into its possession, including those **of the** 'Pious
Fund,' but these latter constituting a trust estate, were of course
taken *cum onere*, **and charged with the** trust. This was fully
recognized **by the Crown, and the** properties **of** the 'Pious
Fund,' **so held in** trust, were thereafter managed in its name by
officers **appointed for the** purpose, called a '*junta directiva.*'
The income and product continued to be **devoted, through the
instrumentality of the Ecclesiastical authorities, to the religious
uses for which** they were dedicated by the **donors.**

"**On the declaration of** Mexican Independence, Mexico suc-
ceeded to the Crown of Spain as trustee of the 'Pious Fund,'
and it continued to be managed, and its income applied as before,
down to September 19, 1836, **when the condition** of the Church

and of the missionary establishments in California seemed to render desirable the erection of the country into a diocese or bishopric, and the selection of a bishop for its government. The Catholic religion being the established religion of Mexico, and it being a known rule of the Holy See not to consent to the erection of new bishoprics in countries acknowledging the Catholic faith, without an endowment from some source adequate to the decent support of the bishopric, the law of the Mexican Congress of September 19, 1836, was passed, which attached an endowment of $6,000 per year to the mitre to be founded, and conceded to the incumbent, when selected, the administration and disposal of the 'Pious Fund.' As it formed the support of the church in his diocese, and the missionaries and their flocks were all his spiritual subjects, and his only ones, this, under the canon law, was a natural result, and its expression merely serves to mark clearly the recognized destination of the fund.

"In pursuance of the invitation held out in this enactment, the two Californias, Upper and Lower, were erected by his Holiness Pope Gregory XVI. into an episcopal diocese, and Francisco Garcia Diego, who had until that time been President of the Missions of Upper California, was made bishop of the newly constituted See ; as such he became entitled to the administration, management and investment of the 'Pious Fund' as trustee, as well as to the application of its income and proceeds to the purposes of its foundation, and for the benefit of his flock.

"On February 8th, 1842, so much of the law of September 19, 1836, as confided the management, investment, etc., of the fund to the bishop, was abrogated by a decree of Santa Anna, then Provisional President of the Republic, and the trust was again devolved on the State ; but that decree did not purport in any way to impugn, impair or alter the rights of the *cestuis que trust* ; on the contrary, it merely devolved on certain government officers the investment and management of the property belonging to the Fund, for the purpose of carrying out the trust established by its donors and founders.

"On October 24th, 1842, another decree was made by the same Provisional President, reciting the inconvenience and unnecessary expense attending the management of the various properties belonging to the ' Pious Fund,' through the medium of public officers, and thereupon directing that the property belonging to it should be sold for the sum represented by its income, (capitalized on the basis of six per cent. per annum), that the proceeds of the sale as well as the cash investments of the fund should be paid into the public treasury, and recognized an obligation on the part of the Government to pay six per cent. per annum on the capital thereof thenceforth.

" In none of these acts, as will be perceived from their language, was there any attempt to destroy or confiscate the property or impair the trust or the rights of the ultimate beneficiaries. On the contrary, the object was distinctly expressed to be more completely and economically to carry out the benevolent intentions of the founders and donors.

" The property of the ' Pious Fund ' at the time of that decree of October 24th, 1842, consisted of real estate, urban and rural, demands on the public treasury for loans theretofore made to the State; moneys invested on mortgage and other security, and the like. A list of these several items, so far as known to the claimants, will be herewith filed as an exhibit. The greater part of the property was sold in pursuance of the last-mentioned decree for a sum of about two millions of dollars of Mexican money, being the equivalent of that sum in gold coin of the United States; the names of the purchasers are not known to the claimants, but are stated by Mr. Duflot de Mofras in his ' *Exploration du Territoire de l'Orégon et des Californies,*' etc., to have been the house of Barnio and Messrs. Rubio Brothers. In the above mentioned sale of the properties of the ' Pious Fund,' the demands existing in its favor on the public treasury for loans to the Government were not included ; the items of the capital of those loans due at the time, so far as they are known to the claimants, will be set forth in the said exhibit. Some of these had preceded the severance of Mexico from the dominions of Spain, but being debts of the viceroyalty of New Spain, were assumed and recognized as debts of the Mexican Republic, as well by the law of June 28th, 1824, as by Article VII. of the Treaty of December 28, 1836, between Mexico and Spain.

" The interest on this capital must, therefore, be added to that on the proceeds of the sale, in ascertaining the arrears of interest due by Mexico to the ' Pious Fund.'

" Whether money debts due by individuals and private corporations to the ' Pious Fund,' (investments on mortgage and the like), were included in the aforesaid sale, or in the sum of two millions of dollars above given as its proceeds, the claimants do not certainly know, but are informed and believe, and therefore charge that they were not, but that those sums were collected by the Mexican Government, they are stated so far as known to the claimants, in said exhibit. The interest on these sums should also be added in ascertaining the arrears of interest now due said fund ; all the sums of money mentioned in said exhibit are in Mexican money, and equivalent to the like sums in gold coin of the United States.

" The Bishop of California remonstrated earnestly against the decree of October 24th, 1842, as a violation of his rights and of the terms of the above law of 1836, those terms were a fundamental condition on which the Holy See had consented to the erection of the bishopric, and therefore had the sacredness of a contract ; and on the 3d of April, 1845, the General Congress passed the Act of that date, restoring to him and his successors, for the purposes of the trust, the properties of the fund yet remaining unsold."

The claim was presented to the Mexican and American Joint Commission at Washington, in the name of the Archbishop and Bishops of the Church of California, representing their flocks, and after considerable litigation, wherein the argument on behalf of the Republic of Mexico was conducted by Hon. Caleb Cushing, subsequently Minister of the United States at the Court of Spain, and Don Manuel Aspiroz, a distinguished Mexican jurisconsult, and lately Consular representative of the Sister Republic in San

Francisco, and by Mr. Doyle on behalf of the claimants, his Excellency Sir Edward Thornton, G. C. B., her Britannic Majesty's Envoy Extraordinary and Minister Plenipotentiary to the United States, rendered his decision, giving to the Church of California a judgment against Mexico for over $900,000. The Commissioners, we are informed, "differed in their judgment, the Mexican Commissioner, Señor de Tamacona, holding that the California Missions were mere political establishments, and the funds provided for their support, no matter whence derived, were merely public funds; while Mr. Wadsworth, the American Commissioner, held the Pious Fund to be a charity of private foundation, and a sacred deposit in the hands of Mexico, which she had no power (and, indeed, had never claimed) to divert to other purposes." "By this difference of opinion," to use the language of a leading non-Catholic journal in this city, "the case of the claimants was practically won, for it could not be supposed that an English publicist of the high character and position of Sir Edward Thornton, could, by a judicial decision, sanction a spoliation of property devoted by its owners to works of piety and charity."

APPENDIX.

Illustrative Notes.

THE LAGUNA [POND] OF DOLORES.

ON page 25 of this volume is the statement: "General Vallejo gives his own, and the authority of the people of ninety years ago, that there used to be a pond, or "small lake," in the Sans Souci Valley, *north* of the Mission Dolores, and immediately behind the hill on which the Protestant Orphan Asylum now stands. It was the common opinion, according to the General, that this was where the expedition halted."

In declining to accept the conclusion of my friend, General Mariano Guadalupe Vallejo, permit me to remark that I have resided here a long time; that neither of us was here in the year 1776, when the Mission was founded; and that I have had ample opportunity to consult the recollection of old people resident here, who received the "traditions of the elders" respecting the early history of San Francisco. The testimony pertinent to that matter is of two kinds—documentary and verbal. Of the documentary:

FIRST.—The statement of Father Francisco Palou, one of the two Franciscan Friars who founded the Mission of Dolores, that on the 27th of June the expedition arrived in the vicinity, and the commander ordered a halt on the margin of a lake (laguna) which Señor Anza named after our Lady of Dolores, "Nuestra Señora de Los Dolores"—(the MATER DOLOROSA of the Roman Catholic Church)—which is in sight of the creek of the Weeping Willows and of the shore of the inlet or arm of that sea which trends to the southeast: "Que esta á la vista de la ensanada de los Lloronas y playa del estero ó brazo del mar que corre al sudeste." (See Palou's *Noticias de la Nueva California*, vol. iv., page 166.) These "Lloronas" (weeping willows) were, of course, not nourished by *salt* water, which would have killed them, but were on the stream of *fresh* water issuing from the ravine lying to the northwest of the Mission church, which supplied the Mission itself and its rancherias with water; and after crossing what are now Valencia, Guerrero, Howard and Folsom streets, emptied into Mission Creek at right angles, at a point about 550 feet easterly from the southeast corner of Folsom and Fourteenth streets; and which, in its whole course, from Mission to Folsom streets, was fringed with "weeping willows," and in full view of the laguna, or pond, which I have designated the Laguna de los Dolores, even as late as the year 1835. The shore of Mission Creek—the arm of that sea which trends to the southeast, the Bay of San Francisco—is also visible from the place which I have designated as the Laguna or Pond of Dolores. Neither of these objects are in sight of the locality in the Sans Souci, where the occasional lake mentioned by General Vallejo existed, but the view of all of them has been, from time immemorial, intercepted by high, intervening hills.

Secondly.—The further statement of the same author, that on the same day and year the expedition encamped on the border of a large pond which empties into that arm of the sea of the port which trends fifteen leagues to the southeast : "Una grande laguna que vacía en el brazo de mar del Puerto que interna quince leguas al sudeste." (*Life of Junípero Serra*, chapter xlv.)

Thirdly.—That when the site of the Mission was selected, it was in the vicinity of that pond, and on the plain lying west of it: "En este mismo sitio de la Laguna, en el plan ó llano que tiene al Poniente." (Palou's *Life of Junípero Serra*, chapter xlv.)

Fourthly.—The fact that when the French Admiral, La Pérouse, touched at Monterey, in September 1786, he dispatched some of his officers to the Port of San Francisco, who made a chart of that Bay, which was sent to France, and published with the account of his explorations up to that point, and is thus preserved to us. On this chart, No. 33 of the series of the maps of

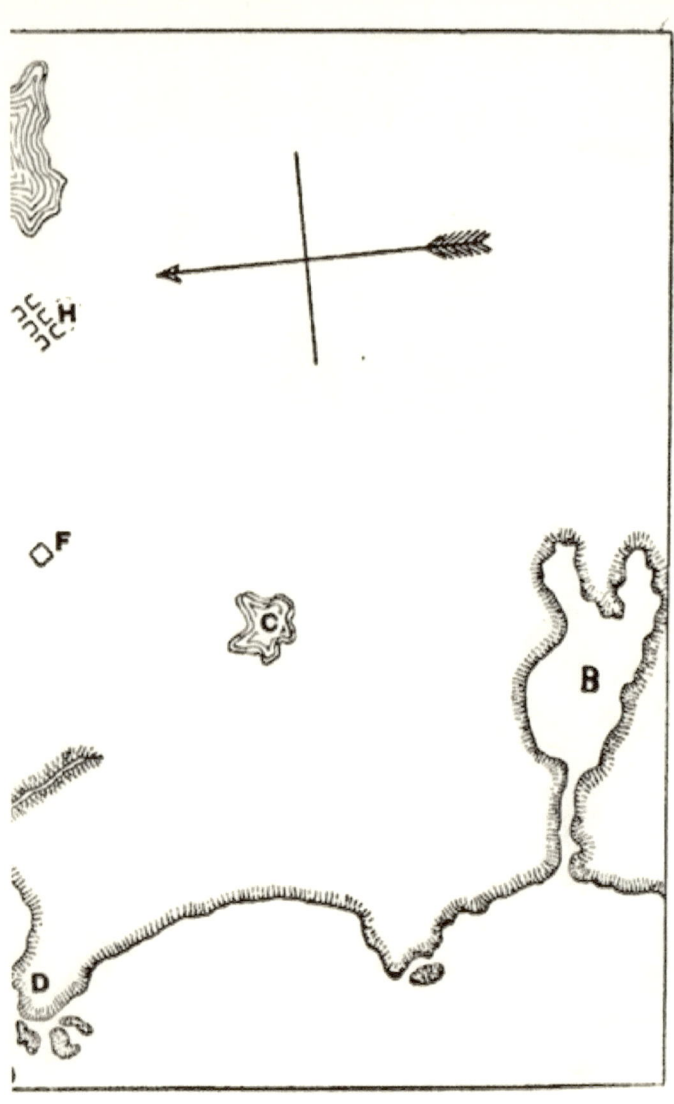

that expedition, (from which a zincographic copy of the Bay of San Francisco is reproduced of the original size on the opposite page,) although it is not hydrographically accurate in respect of mathematical proportions and distances, as, of course, it could not be, without an actual survey; yet the general lines of the coast and of the Bay, and the relative positions of the prominent physical objects, are laid down with a wonderful approximation to correctness. "La Laguna de los Dolores" [1] is laid down precisely where the "Willows" were situated, with an outlet into that portion of the Bay of San Francisco "which trends towards the southeast," answering precisely to the description given by Palou. It is ten times as large as "Washer-woman's Lagoon;" [G] which is called "Pequeña Laguna"— little pond—and is five times as large as Mountain Lake [C] "La Laguna del Presidio"--Presidio Pond. It is curious and interesting to observe that, while Alcatraz [J] and Angel Island [K] have their respective modern designations, Yerba Buena Island [M] is called, "La Isla del Carmel"—Carmel Island; Fort Point [D] "La Punta del Angel de la Guarda"--the Point of the Guardian Angel; Point Lobos is not named, although it and its Seal Rocks are laid down; and the "Laguna de la Merced" [B] is represented as having a free, open communi-cation with the ocean.

The Presidio [F] and also the Mission [H] are designated on the plan. Thus, in the year 1786, and only ten years after the Mission of Dolores was founded, a *corps* of French naval officers, coming to San Francisco with instructions to make a map of the localities here, do make one, which, on its face, bears testimony to its general correctness, and on which a laguna or pond, called the Laguna of Dolores, is laid down, and . also the Mission of Dolores, precisely where Palou says it was, "to the west of the said Laguna, and on the same plain."

Thus far with the documentary testimony.

Now, as to the verbal testimony. Some twelve years ago I had an interview with a well-known lady, then resident at the Mission of Dolores, Doña Carmen Sibrian de Bernal. She was born of Spanish lineage, in Monterey, California, in the year 1804; was married at San José in 1821, to José Cornelio Bernal, a resident of the Mission of Dolores, and they came there to reside in the same year. She was a woman of great vivacity, and stated to me that the tradition given to her by the old residents of the Mission was, that when the Missionary Fathers came here to establish the Mission, they encamped at a pond which existed where the place of resort, called the " Willows," was at the time of this interview, to which a great tide creek formerly made up from the Bay : " Eu donde son ahora los Saucelitos, en donde habia en eso tiempo un estero grande de la Bahia." I also, at that time, visited the site of the " Willows," and found that although the soil had been greatly filled in during my own recollection by the deposits of silt and of vegetable accretions, the fresh water was still flowing out towards the Bay; and I could not find any tree there which appeared to be more than forty years old. The " estero," or tide creek still made up nearly to "the Willows," but I then thought that it must soon be obliterated by the progress of public improvements.

Since the date of that interview the tract embracing "the Willows," and included within Seventeenth, Nineteenth, Valencia and Howard streets, has been graded and filled in; but from the sewers which drain it there still flows a constant stream of clear fresh water, showing that the Laguna was fed by living springs.

The laguna or pond which General Vallejo mentions was in a shallow, natural basin, in a sandy soil. It was only an occasional body of water, not fed by springs, but wholly by the winter rains, and dried up early in the summer. It was situated on the old road leading from the Mission to the Presidio, and lay to the southwest of the old place of resort, called Sans Souci. It was only a shallow, spoon-shaped hollow, receiving in ordinary seasons not rains enough to overflow its borders, but only sufficient to raise a thin crop of *cañutales*, or reeds, which, as the water dried up, were supplanted by a growth of native grasses. This body of water, from the time when I arrived in San Francisco, in October, 1849, to the present date, never attained any historical dimensions until the memorable rainy winter of 1861–62. Then the seven windows of the heavens were opened, and this hollow in the sandy plain was not only filled up, but overflowed. The narrow lip of sand which formed its easterly boundary is cut through, either by natural or artificial means; a thin stream thus finds an outlet—" *Vires acquiret eundo*"—becomes a vast torrent, sweeping to the Bay; bears havoc and destruction in its front, and leaves innumerable beneficent lawsuits in its rear. But that this accidental and occasional Laguna, such as it was, situated at the *northwest* of the Mission of Dolores, with intervening ranges of broken hills and valleys, was the Laguna situate to the *east* of the Mission, on the same plain, let those believe who can. My opinion is that the "Willows" and the Pond or Laguna of Dolores, were one and the same.

SIR FRANCIS DRAKE'S BAY.

In my address, at page 81, of this volume, speaking of the condition of California at a period not far remote, I said:

" One hundred and seven years ago, in the year 1769, California was a desert wilderness. Its coasts had been explored by Spanish navigators, who had given names to its prominent points, but throughout its vast territory, more than 800 miles in extent from south to north, there was no cabin or tent of the white man, no vestige of his presence, no physical trace of his existence. The bay of San Francisco, the most marked and marvellous feature in the northwestern line of the continent, had not been discovered. A delusive cloud generally brooded over the entrance of the Golden Gate, like the magic mist obscuring the entrance to the treasures of an oriental fable. Even Sir Francis Drake, who, in the year 1578, after having committed piratical plunder upon the Spanish galleons bearing the treasures of the kings of Spain from Manilla to Acapulco, fled to the north, hoping to escape the vengeance of his pursuers by finding and navigating a northeast passage to the Atlantic Ocean, sailed ignorantly across the vast volume of the Sacramento and San Joaquin rivers discharging themselves into the ocean athwart the very keel of his caravel, and whose existence, if known to him, would have suggested to him that he had found the overland water passage of which he was in search."

I said this purposely, as a deliberate protest against the notion that Sir Francis Drake ever entered the Bay of San Francisco. I have thoroughly examined, collated, indexed and digested all the historical evidences which exist relating to that subject matter, and I am satisfied that they do not show that Sir Francis Drake ever visited or even heard of the Bay of San Francisco. This Centennial celebration was a proper occasion for the protest; and I regret that a discussion of the question which I am preparing cannot be published with this note. It may very probably appear in a subsequent edition of this book.

JOHN W. DWINELLE.

www.ingramcontent.com/pod-product-compliance
Lightning Source LLC
Chambersburg PA
CBHW020612030726
47497CB00007B/2199